Americans in Paradise

by

Michael Lin Baum

© 2001, 2011 by Michael Lin Baum

Americans in Paradise
0-9715132-0-1

Published by
And This, Too Press
Tarzana, CA 91356

Edited and Designed by
Words & Pictures Press
Dunedin, FL 34698
www.wordsandpicturespress.com

Buddhahood is not to be realized externally, but internally, as being from beginningless time a natural characteristic of mind; one need not seek outside oneself, for Buddhahood is already innate in one, and only awaits the removal of avidya (ignorance) *to shine forth like the Sun when the clouds are dissipated.*

— from The Tibetan Book of
the Great Liberation

It is easy to go down into Hell...; but to climb back again, to retrace one's steps to the upper air — there's the rub...

— from Virgil's Aeneid

"All I wanted was a Pepsi, just one Pepsi."

— from "Institutionalized"
by Suicidal Tendencies

TABLE OF CONTENTS

*From Ritual
To Romance*

BERNIE got out of the sack early because Vi's back was acting up again. He stumbled down the hall in his p.j.'s, still retaining bits of the dream from which he had just arisen. And he was still retaining them when he kicked the kitchen door. After wearily condemning its existence, and proceeding into the kitchen, he turned on the lights and began gathering for breakfast. He paused to shout to Vilma, asking her what she wanted for breakfast.

"Nothing? You want nothing? What sort of a way is that for an invalid to act? You eat. Now what do you want?"

"I don't want nothing, Bernard."

"What's that you say? I can't hear you—you want eggs?"

"Yes I want eggs . . . Fix me eggs."

The house was quiet except for the muffled sounds of Bernie's searching. Vilma crawled out of the bed onto two magazines and a slipper. She groaned all the way to the toilet, releasing a decisive sigh of relief upon reaching it.

"Vilma, where the hell is the cooking grease?"

"Oh my God, Bernard, can't you leave me alone long enough to relieve myself?"

"What's that you said Vilma? It's in the refrigerator?"

Vi pulled herself up, wondering what she ever did to deserve a deaf schlemiel that could not even cook eggs without getting his finger stuck up his toches. She calmly opened the bathroom door, immediately becoming aware of the dusky disarray of the bedroom. She stepped over two damp purple towels, moved the chair with all the magazines and newspapers collected over the weekend, and began heading towards the bedroom door.

She dramatically entered the hall, throwing the door open and marching out onto the new carpeting. She waddled methodically, with anticipation. Her hands came down to her sides. Her lips pursed.

Bernard was stirring, he somehow felt Vilma approaching. He, too, let his hands drop to his sides and shuffled toward the kitchen door.

Then they stopped: frozen, waiting, watching. Bernard was fat. He had not shaved. His stomach flabbed over his pajama bottoms, his flat feet swelled over the sides of his house sandals, his nose was pinched from his glasses and his breathing was loud from his asthma. Vi was no better. Her permanent was lopsided, eye makeup had oozed into her crow's feet, her varicose veins seemed black against her sickly skin, and her face was wrinkled and puffy from having just gotten out of bed. Her breasts and hips were obscured by the robe that went down to her knees.

They met in all the cadaverous beauty of morning glory. Bernard smiled a weak smile and Vilma frowned a superior frown, each of them expressing themselves superbly. And it was a perfect day for superb self-expression. The sun shone that peculiar, glareless haze that one sees reflected off burnished metal or the undersides of leaves before a storm, a sort of sublime clarity that forebodes a nuclear disaster or a superb day for self-expression. Bernard took the initiative and claimed that the cooking oil was not in the refrigerator, and as a matter of fact, there wasn't any cooking oil in the whole goddamn house.

"What are you, crazy, Bernard? Why would anyone put cooking oil in the refrigerator? There, Bernard, there it is right in the corner."

Bernard was not about to believe any of this, and before looking, asked, "Where?"

He then looked, and over in the corner was a can of Crisco cooking oil.

"Oh, I thought I was looking for a bottle."

"Hmhm."

Vilma waddled back to the toilet and Bernard smacked some Crisco into the pan. He had left the burner on too hot and the grease splattered all over—most notably through his pajamas, prompting a cry of "Holy Shit!"

"Bernard, none of that language in this house!"

Which, of course, he did not hear.

About an hour later, Bernard had finished breakfast, showered, shaved and dressed. He had his hearing aid on and was apparently ready for work. Vilma decided to stay home. She would not be able to type all day with her coccyx deteriorating right out from under her.

"Bernard, did you fix yourself a lunch?"

"What are you, crazy or something? Of course I fixed a lunch. You want I should starve?"

"That wasn't called for, Bernard."

"All right, all right. Goodbye."

"Hmhm. Goodbye."

Bernie closed the door as the goodbye faded. He was off to work. As a traveling electrical supplies salesman, he wandered around upstate New York's factory districts, taking orders from his list of established customers. His job could probably have been performed by phone, but he had discovered early on that linking his line of light bulbs, fluorescent lamps and lighting fixtures to the pornographic knick-knacks he bestowed with each order fostered a recurring subliminal desire to re-order, thus loyal customers. The knick-knacks required personal delivery.

Bernie spent the morning visiting the purchasers for a ball bearing plant and an air conditioner manufacturer, leaving them with some pens that exposed a nude photo of Marilyn Monroe when tipped upright. He then stopped off at a fishing spot to pass lunch.

He sat half-in and half-out the right side of his mud-brown Chrysler, holding in his lap the handle of a Garcia rod and reel which he had found up at Wellesley Island the previous summer. He had the fishing line strung out over a small bridge into what was obviously heavily polluted water. The sun warmed him and he started to relax, pulling his fishing hat down and leaning into a pillow propped against the driver's side door. A sparkling gold reflection off the water kept him awake, giving his eyes something to focus on.

He had just started to doze off when he remembered to eat lunch. He straightened up, carefully setting the Garcia rod down, then turned to the lunch box under his seat . . . and to his surprise, there was a sandal. Then two sandals. With feet. Then a robe and a man—white, all white. A man sitting in the car, wearing a flowing white robe and beat-up sandals. Bernard flinched, dropping the lunch box and knocking the rear view mirror with his head. He was too surprised to say anything; his mouth could just hang open.

After several seconds of posing with his mouth open, Bernie's immediate fear subsided, and he took a closer look at the man in the driver's seat. Bernie peered at him, with his right eyebrow cocked. He saw a man, obviously Jesus Christ. At least he sure as hell looked like all those pictures of Jesuses with blue eyes gazing at some horizon, dripping with sincerity. He was Christ alright . . . he glowed . . . glowed white.

"Who the hell are you?"

"Jesus Christ."

"Hmhm."

Bernie watched him, relaxed and watched for five or so minutes. Just sat there looking at this guy Jesus H. Christ, thinking, "What the hell would Vilma say?"

VILMA was sitting in bed with a True Romance beside her and a New Yorker in her lap, the covers pulled over her knees. She had been reading for an hour or so an article by Charles Sangerman on Elijah Grey, the true inventor of the telephone. She was getting bored, thinking of being in the office, thinking she should be at the office, she should really be typing, but then she shifted her rear and reminded herself of her deteriorating coccyx. She still thought she ought to . . . there was a man in the doorway. A man in the doorway stood with his hands folded in front of him, resting them on his stomach.

She jerked up, slapping her hands at her sides, as if to escape, as if pushing the bed with her arms would propel her away from him. He just stood there with a pious smile, glowing a hazy white and being patient.

She was frightened—shaking but immovable, unable to shout or scream or hide. Her eyes bulged for minutes, but gradually relaxed after she realized that he was not planning a sneak attack, and probably was not even planning to rape her. She sat in the bed watching this hermaphroditic fluorescence standing in the doorway.

VILMA'D think he was crazy, that's what she'd think.

What if I'm dead?

"Am I dead?"

"No, not yet." Christ smiled sympathetically.

"What sort of an answer is that? Not yet!" Bernie laughed to himself. "You know, we don't subscribe to your religion."

"Oh." Christ disappeared, leaving no trace.

Bernard stared at the place where Jesus Christ had just been. He wondered, What sort of a thing would cause a hallucination like that? A "Christianity striking at the Jews" complex? A complex. Yes, that must be it, a complex. Then I'm crazy. No I'm not. It was a figment of my imagination. A daydream. A complex. Was it my fault that he left? What sort of talk is this? Crazy talk.

The pole jumped and so did Bernie. Some fish was taking off with the bobber. Some fish that had managed to live in that water swallowed Bernie's hook, and Bernie started reeling him in.

"Goddamn fish . . . a fishie ha ha. . . . I got you, you little bastard . . ."

And he did. A bluegill about eight inches long with a hook through its eye.

[7]

"Goddamn . . . now what am I going to do with you? You little sucker . . . what'd you go and get the hook stuck in your juiced up little eye for?"

He pulled the hook out and threw the fish back in the water. He reeled the line the rest of the way in, threw it in the back seat, and started the car, off to another bunch of customers.

MEANWHILE, Vilma Seigal was still in bed, covers over her knees, staring at the man standing in the doorway. For fifteen minutes she sat there watching this dazzling white, yes, man, standing with a damn smirk on his face.

No, he wasn't smirking, he understood. He understood her pain. He knew, yes, that was his smile.

"Would you like some coffee?" she asked.

"Yes."

Vi rose, remembering not to forget her coccyx, and walked towards the man. She thought of asking him to fix her, to make her healthy. She thought of seducing him. She was afraid to look at his eyes, afraid that he might know.

When she reached him, she smiled sheepishly, not knowing what she was to do. He did not say anything, but made way for her to escort him to the kitchen.

Vi was embarrassed by the mess she was expecting to find. And there it was, all over the dining table and furniture: cigar boxes, knitting bags, trash, mail, a wadded pile of nylons, a girdle with a hole worn through the rear. She smiled to him again, trying to excuse the inhospitality of their unnecessary squalor. He was still smiling, as if amused by her anxiety, and not really interested or even seeing any of the litter.

By the time they reached the kitchen, Vi was not aware of her back. She invited him to sit down in one of her purple dining chairs. Vilma had something about the color purple, and was suddenly aware of its gaudiness in the presence of what she was sure was Christ's radiance.

Bernard had left a kitchen mess which she cleaned up for several minutes before preparing the coffee. She sat down across from her guest while waiting for the coffee to perk. She was not sure whether to look up in his eyes—what would happen if she did—so she looked down, her eyes occasionally drifting over to his hand, which was resting on the table. He was relaxed, the other hand in his lap; he was relaxed and leaning back in the chair; he was relaxed, but alert. He overflowed with politeness and self-assured humility. The archangels had apparently fed him better than the icons had indicated.

Vi was aware of her Jewishness, of her not believing in Christ.

But how could that be? Here he was. Right at her table, waiting to drink coffee. Coffee—black or white? Probably black. Yes, most assuredly black. Are there TV shows like this? No, of course not. Yes—on Sunday mornings, just before the Polish Polka hour . . . yes, these things happen . . . it's OK. Yes.

"Oh my god the coffee!"

She got up and poured coffee for the two of them, not aware of the faux pas she had just uttered.

But Christ still just sat there. She turned, with the coffee in her hands, and inadvertently looked into his eyes, forgetting that he was not just any guest over for coffee.

She was absorbed—consumed—by a fantasia of radiance, something like falling through a large golden cloud of intense pleasure. Beatitude. An ecstasy beyond all dreams of sensuality. She had been relieved, relieved beyond all pain, overcome. . . .

BERNARD came home early. With the shades drawn closed, the house was dark except for a light on in the kitchen. He set his briefcase down with a loud thump and collapsed on the sofa, trying to figure out how to describe to Vilma what had happened.

Vilma was lying in the kitchen, coffee stains all over the lavender carpeting. There were two cups, one on either side of her.

The handle of the one on the left had been broken. Bernard's entrance roused her. She got up, instinctively bracing her back. She glanced around, surprised at finding herself in the kitchen, alarmed at the coffee stains she had been lying in. She moved around the kitchen, with her hand on her back, limping. Then she effortlessly straightened and began cleaning the mess with a quiet smile.

*Christopher's
Initiation*

ON the evening of October 23, a dreamlike intensity pervaded Christopher Graham's house. The Grahams were having a party. It was serving as both a housewarming and an unofficial gathering for the members of Mr. Graham's department at work. As cars from different towns in the surrounding area began to arrive, the old farmhouse lost some of the hollowness it had when too few people were living in it.

It had not snowed yet and most of the leaves were still on the trees that bordered the farmyard. Some of the fields around the house had not been harvested, though a dull brown on the crops showed they were well past being ready. The tractor path to the back fields was strewn with yellow and orange leaves, dead weeds, and ears of corn that had dropped from the trailer. Couples remarked that the sunset was very pretty through the dark branches and leaves. A pale gold reflection washed whatever blemishes the brilliant daylight had revealed, and the sky was set with a pink that blended with the various orange, gold and turquoise hues of an evening approaching twilight.

The guests entered through the front door and Mr. Graham greeted them with a show of hospitality and friendliness that somehow did not relay a sense of well-being to the newcomers, but rather a snide hostility which he was incapable of controlling. He took their coats and offered them a punch laced with rum. The first room they entered was a dining room dimly lit by some candles and a brass chandelier hanging over the dinner table. There were several paintings on the walls, most of them simply travel posters placed in wood frames. One was an oil of Mrs. Graham's from before their marriage. Several people walked around the table choosing from the buffet Mrs. Graham had prepared.

Middle-aged women, needlessly fat, picked at the oysters, crackers, strip steak, chopped frankfurters and fruit jellos. Many began drinking immediately and continued to do so until a fatuous daze glazed their faces.

Christopher had introduced himself to the first few guests and had entertained several of the men with a game of pool, which he won. He was asked several times if he was the bright young man going away to the university so early. An older woman, already visibly drunk, drifted over to him saying, "Oh, you must be the one I read about. You remind me so much of my son."

She leaned on the balustrade, allowing Christopher to watch her breasts calculatingly swell over the yoke of her black crepe gown. They lacked tension and seemed to sag from a weariness she disguised in creams and supports. He noticed the tired skin around her eyes and the limp quality of her cheeks beneath several layers of make-up and rouge. She wanted him to talk to her.

"Are you Christopher?"

"Yes."

"You must be an awfully bright boy."

"No," he said, "just an overachiever."

She started to speak again, but was interrupted by another woman, who walked over saying, "Martha, it's been so long since I've seen you."

"Oh, Margaret! How are you?"

They guided each other across the room to a seat and Christopher caught bits of their conversation as they moved away. He heard "quiet" and "hospital" and "leukemia." He watched them talk to each other with their drinks in their hands and their cigarettes in their ashtrays. Then his attention went over the rest of the party. Some men were drunk enough to start singing "Salvation Army." A small crowd of people circled them and laughed.

"Salvation Army! Salvation Army!

"Put a nickel on the drum, save another drunken bum.

"Salvation Army! Salvation Army!"

One ruddy-complexioned, athletic-looking man turned over a basket to use as a drum and began singing:

"I used to drink!!!"

"Boo!" the crowd reproved.

"I used to swear!"

"Boo!"

"I used to go out with wild, wild women!!"

"Boo!!" they shouted loudly.

"Now I don't drink!"

"Yea!"

"Now I don't swear!"

"Yea!!"

"Now I don't go out with wild, wild women!!

"All I do is sit here beating on this goddamned drum!!!"

"Yea!!!!" they yelled, and laughed and fell over each other.

And they sang more rounds as more people came and more people sang. Christopher continued looking at the party. Everyone talked at someone, and, except for occasional bits of phrases, it seemed like one large, incomprehensible noise. He watched people talking without hearing anything they said. Their mouths moved, but their eyes seemed dazed and preoccupied. He heard of arthritis and toilets and television and punch lines to jokes about genitals and feces. Some people were sitting on the floor. He knew his father was, by now, in the kitchen sitting on the floor, his face red and his eyes watery.

Christopher felt the beginning of a headache and decided to go upstairs where it was less noisy. No one noticed that he was slipping away and he felt a sort of mischievous pleasure that he could slip away so easily. As he reached the top of the stairs, he looked out an uncurtained window and saw two more guests arriving, a man and a woman. The woman was tall and wore a bright yellow coat that seemed almost luminescent in the half dusk. She looked like she might be very pretty, and he considered going back down the stairs to meet her, but he had an image of her being dull and talking about Siamese cats or getting her hair done, so he continued on his escape to his room.

He walked in without turning on the light. The room was not completely dark. From the hall light outside his room he could see the writing on some of the posters over his desk. He sat on his bed looking at them. Some of them he had painted himself; some he had bought at a poster and candle shop. He recalled an evening spent on one poster, on which he had written in oriental script:

"We fly in the streams of a new dynasty. Watch for signs."

He regarded it with an ironic admiration. He did not think of new dynasties, or mystical signs, but rather the phrase "We fly in the streams . . ." He had seen the quote in an underground paper and thought it was so peculiar that he turned it over and over in his mind. A few months later he made the poster during a burst of interior decorating. He had painted an oriental vase with bamboo shoots in it and then spontaneously decided to paint the quote over it, resulting in what he thought was a very clever poster.

During this reverie, the beginning of a song ran through his head and he tried to pin it down. He caught it and let it play for a while. It was from a soundtrack he had given as a gift to his first girlfriend. As he listened to his image of it, he felt a poignant wave of sadness, not directly from the song—it was a more or less cheerful and poetic song—but from the ambience in which he last listened to it. He noted the trace of sorrow and distinguished it as separate from the mood of the song itself. He found this curious and pondered over the subtle influence a previous emotion could have on his subjective feelings much later. He found it interesting, perhaps even alarming, that his emotional attitude during the song was dictated not by what the song intended to stir in his imagination, but by the general feeling from the circumstances in which he was involved at that time. It was a sort of deception. He wondered whether, if he continuously heard the song, he would have this feeling as a general state of mind, including the feeling of reticence with girls which accompanied it. What he found novel was that something innocuous in the present subliminally activated an entire state of mind. He speculated on this for several minutes and submitted to the poignant sadness again before deciding to actually listen to the song. He reached over to his collection at the end of his bed and tried to find it, but the room was too dark; he had to get up and turn on the light.

The bright, yellowish light changed the entire atmosphere of his room. The colors of the posters became less subtle, and the clothes, books and papers lying around his bed came out of hiding and disturbed the harmonious feeling the darkened room had given him. He wanted to turn the light back off, but left it on to find the song. There was an unfinished letter lying on his desk, which he picked up as he went back to the albums. He leafed through the collection, found the soundtrack, and put it on his stereo. Christopher turned on a reading light and turned off the overhead light. The music began as he pulled two pillows under his head and stretched out on the bed. He reread the letter he had picked up, then rolled over to get a pen and a clipboard.

He enjoyed writing letters. He drew on them, wrote in rhythm to music, wrote in different handwriting styles, and tried endless other amusements. This letter was already several pages long, and within a short while, several more pages had been added to it. The album had ended without his noticing. He reviewed the letter once more, correcting it twice, folded it and put it in an envelope, then threw it on his desk with a note of finality.

He rose from the bed, feeling a little hungry, and decided to sneak back downstairs. The voices and clinking of glasses grew louder as he approached the stairs. He could see the party was now moving through a thick haze of cigarette smoke. As he came down to the party, he singled out the yellow-coated girl, or was it woman, whom he had categorized, encysted and ejected from his memory just an hour before. He half tried to avoid her, but she walked straight up to him, closer than he would have expected.

"How do you do? My name is Judith. You're Christopher, if I'm not mistaken."

He nodded. He thought she was too drunk.

"Christ am I drunk. Your father . . . your father snuck much too much rum into that punch." She raised a large tumbler, nearly full.

Christopher half smiled.

"You're the son, aren't you? The one in the paper? I've been trying to find you all night. I was afraid you'd skipped out, and here I'd be, deserted with all these—these Philistines, my one chance of meeting *someone* gone. A slim chance, mind you, but one's driven to desperate hopes at affairs like this."

He was a little embarrassed. He did not feel particularly non-Philistine himself, and was afraid she would soon find out her overestimation.

"You were hiding, weren't you—my god, hold me up—yes you were hiding. I would have, too. They're so *stupid*—virtually illiterate, except for what TV spoon-feeds them. Here, have some punch." She held out the tumbler, adding, "You read, don't you?"

Nodding, he accepted the glass and took a couple of gulps. Her vivacity eclipsed the rest of the party, and he was already more or less awed by her.

"Well, what sort of things do you read?" Judith asked.

"Oh, you know—uh, Herman Hesse . . . Salinger, Thomas Mann. That sort of thing. Or when I'm feeling especially self-possessed, I'll attempt Dostoyevsky—"

"Why 'self-possessed?'"

He'd half-expected to be interrupted; she did not seem like the type that would let him get away so easily with that sort of name-dropping.

"Oh, uh, he's so—uh—he dissects, systematically dissects whatever ego or sense of self-worth I can muster. *Notes from Underground* was rough, but *The Double*—Christ! I don't know, it was just short of . . . traumatic."

"Yes, he is the double-edged sword, isn't he? You love to read him, but it's so painful. He had such an undaunted insight into the despicable elements of our psyches. You read him and see so much of your dirty linen splattered all over the page that you begin to see all of your motivations as fundamentally vile, but it's really not so. The self-inspection doesn't hurt any, though. It's good for you. Have you read Nietzsche, too? No, perhaps you're too young. Now *Siddhartha*, that was just beautiful . . . poetic, wasn't it?"

Her face seemed to glow, though it was really the reflection of candlelight on her skin and around her hair. Christopher examined her more closely, defining more precisely his impression of her being attractive. She was tall and slim, nearly as tall as he was. Her eyes were large and appeared to be a dark blue or black in the candlelight. She seemed flamboyant and striking and self-assured. Her eyes were direct and washed him with a warmth she seemed to emanate. He noticed that her lips were moist, that her hand held her glass carelessly, that the fingers were long and the skin looked soft and warm. She was talking about perfunctory Christians, insipidness and her husband.

She smiled and said, "I'm attractive. I don't fool myself into thinking I'm not. Don't let my husband see us talking—he'll be jealous. He's sitting on the kitchen floor with your father making a complete ass of himself, a job he does only half as well when he's sober." She took his hand and whispered into his ear, "Here, hold me up while I show you off."

And Christopher was swept away into the smoky din of the living room with Judith clinging to him. She'd been right about the punch. He was becoming drunk with her: drunk from her including him in her circle of being versus non-being, drunk from the pressure of her body against his side, from her admiration, from her insight, and from the glow surrounding her as they drifted through dozens of vapid conversations. She seemed to know his thoughts better than he himself, and was able to express them more articulately. Surrounding them was a sea of dull faces, while she remained lucid, even luminescent. There never seemed to be any end to what they could discuss, and there never seemed to be any limit to what she would divulge. After a while, she warmed into something on the order of a lecture.

"Well, I don't consider them to be innocuous. Beneath their veils of smiles and deodorants are self-protective, calculating designs that have very little to do with what is good or noble or virtuous. Take them out of the confines of society's laws and mores, and you'll have beasts—savage animals. The veiled intents, the disguised implications, would . . . would become realities. These people with their vulvas and penises wouldn't be joking about rape or murder or perversions," she said quietly in his ear. "This guy wouldn't be just looking down her dress, he'd have her half-conscious under some bushes, biting her bare nipple. And she would probably be loving it. Her husband . . . her husband here wouldn't joke about protecting his honor, he'd grab the nearest rock and smash his skull into a pulp and then leave the head on a pike outside their cave to remind her. There wouldn't just be jealousy and envy. There'd be robbery and plunder. Beneath these smiles I see something I don't like. I'm not deceived by these manners. They're chained, but not docile. Freud, Nietzsche, Schopenhauer understood these things.

"And the thing is, they don't have to be this way. They lack the will, the temerity, for any of thousands of reasons, to face the cesspool that compels them and . . . and transcend it. Self-evolution, self-elevation, or whatever, alternates between suffering and accomplishment. And it's too easy not to do it. So here they are: stupid, superficial, and complacent, driven by impulses and desires they don't know the source of, their only claim to sanity a fragile veil of manners and inhibitions.

"A truly civilized man's mores have been inspected, re-evaluated, and kept or discarded according to his concept of . . . paradise."

She interrupted herself, then clicked her tongue and sighed.

"Look at me, I'm running off at the mouth like an adolescent lush. Not your model of perfection, eh?" She brought her hand to her forehead and winced. "Ooh . . . I'm going to have to sit down—this punch is positively poisonous. Take me someplace quiet—not too quiet or I might not be able to keep myself from seducing you, but someplace quiet."

She was nearly limp on his shoulder. He still had her punch glass in one hand. The other hand was around her waist to hold her up. The subtle fragrance of her perfume was, to him, like the gentle scent of irises in spring. With her, he felt, he could be anywhere. This party could last forever. Her thoughts crystallized his vague attitudes. He felt certainty and confidence where there had just been cloudy notions and nebulous feelings. He wanted to tell her how beautiful she was, but somehow could not.

He led her through the periphery of the party to an enclosed patio that had been added to the back of the old house. It was a cool room warmed only by its proximity to the house. In another month it would have been too cold without a room heater. The two of them sat on a couch in front of some windows facing the fields behind the house. The noise and chatter of the party could barely be made out, except for occasional squeals of laughter or surprise. For several minutes they sat looking out the windows. It was very dark. The forms of unlit buildings and groups of trees eerily reflected the starlight. Their shapes seemed to possess a primeval force undetectable in daylight. Christopher noted the same quality in Judith's figure spread over the corner of the couch. Without the multiplicity of visual details provided by light, his imagination was empowered to fill in. He noted the symmetry of her arm curved across the top of the couch. This curve was balanced by the angle of her wrist as her hand edged over the top of the pillow.

Judith said, as if voicing his thoughts, "I think the imagination is flooded by too much sensory information. We become distracted by so much flotsam and jetsam that the world becomes solid, inflexible, unyielding to our fancy. I think objective reality is inversely proportional to imagination. The mind, flooded with so much superfluous information, especially at the lightning pace of today's society, lacks the capacity to empower the imagination.

"Some things allow our imagination to prevail over reality. Doorways to the nether world. Like twilight. Like this. Look how beautiful we are, and the trees. Under the influence of drugs, art and twilight, the imagination is unchained. And maybe in love, too. What am I talking about now? I'm too drunk to remain coherent for more than one sentence straight. But I know that's what the Buddhists talked about—we're distracted by our hyperactive senses. You see?"

Christopher muttered, "Hm-hmm."

Throughout her speech, he continued to study the symmetry of her body, the angle of her neck and head to the curve of her shoulder, the sweep of her waist to her hips. It was only the forms and dimensions he perceived, not the surface, not the image. He wondered if this raw beauty was the realm of Plato's forms. He thought about the possibility of her speech patterns possessing the same sort of geometric assemblage. He flirted with the notion that these patterns themselves, the geometric relationships of thought and body, were what actually drew people together, that they had similar or complementary geometric arrangements. He expanded the notion to a theory of personal interaction, proved by the fact that people who lived together a long time tended to look alike—people and their dogs, Ozzie and Harriet. They complemented or duplicated each other's geometric assemblages. Then he thought about Judith, about her dark shadow-like form, her resonant voice. He felt as if he were perceiving the core of Judith, the essence of Judithness. Perhaps her soul. He recognized he was a little drunk too, but transported, not plowed under. He had almost forgotten there was a party going on somewhere nearby. He saw the soft curve of her calf and the delicate ankle. He wondered how so much beauty—Judith, the trees, the stars—could all have happened by the random combination of infinitely small, infinitely multitudinous, infinitely random particles of energy and matter. How could this happen by chance? Not their meeting, but that they existed at all. He pondered over this mystery as she mentioned the Buddhists. And the word "Buddhist" was like a trigger, as if it were the key word, hanging in the space-time continuum waiting to be mentioned. He felt a spark of insight, a sudden sense of rightness. He saw his life and all his experience, he saw the universe in a ball all pass before him, all seen completely and understood as imagination versus reality, spirit versus matter. He saw in each detail of his life this divine struggle. For a moment he rested in awe of this image. He watched it shimmer, scintillate, then fade. He saw Judith again, whose eyes seemed to be closed. He saw her beautiful and original and unaffected and felt a rush of affection for her which, in the divine scheme of things, was proper and pure, therefore not requiring restraint.

He thought she might be just filling in the silence, waiting for him to seduce her. Assuming this, he became embarrassed over his reticence, yet inhibited by the possibility that he was merely misinterpreting his conception of the ambience. He ran through a number of gestures and phrases that would suavely bridge the chasm he was about to cross, anxious against shattering the rapport they had created. He wanted to find the right means of communicating the feeling she aroused in him. He began to see it as a problem of communication and understanding, not seduction and respect, but then thought that that thought might merely have been a justification for lacking the courage to seduce her. He felt trapped by his own logic. A moment earlier, he had been set free of restraint, but now he was caught in the web of confused motives and imagination. He felt pressed to assert his sexuality. When he noted this pressure, he saw it as distinct from the feeling she aroused then, at that time. He felt the same intimation of self-deception as he had sensed earlier with the song in his room. Discarding the inapposite impulse, he could clearly see Judith and the rapport between them. He was calm and felt a genuine, untainted fondness. He reached for her hand and held it in his two hands, stroking the smooth, warm skin of her fingers, but before he could speak, he heard someone calling "Judith!" from the distant clatter of the party.

"Oh Christ, it's Stuart!"

They both stood simultaneously and moved toward the doorway. Someone turned on the light from inside the house. The room suddenly became smaller and cluttered with lawn chairs, unused lamps, bed frames, storm windows and window screens. The room was dusty and the tattered pillows of the couch now became visible. All this was absorbed in a glance as Judith's husband stumbled in.

"Judith, it's time for us to go." His voice sounded like his tongue was thick and heavy in his mouth. His face, though flushed and puffy, was insipidly handsome. His sudden presence in the room acted like a powerful magnet to their startled attention. The minute details of his face and eyes, his straight, brown hair, and his disheveled clothes were all magnified under their surprised stares. Christopher felt like he was cut off from time, like a kite suddenly cut from its string, floating in free space before it begins its inevitable plunge to the earth. Stuart looked suspiciously at Christopher, then Judith, and apparently satisfied himself that nothing was amiss.

Seeing this, Judith responded immediately, "That's fine, Stuart. Where's my coat?"

From a distance, Christopher noted how easily Stuart's attention was diverted away from him and the patio back to the house and going home.

Stuart motioned toward the front of the house. "Back where you left it." He turned around as he spoke and said the last few words with his back turned to them. Judith accompanied him through the door and Christopher followed. As they walked through the intervening rooms to the living room, Christopher began to wonder how Judith could be married to someone so dull. His mind began to race. It rushed through images of Judith, young and naïve, and Stuart, initially charming and dominating, their marriage, the incipient disparity and boredom, a teacher's voice and the phrase, "appearances can be deceiving." He saw them fighting and separating. He saw Stuart sullen, watching television and reading Hemingway at the same time. He saw them walking ahead of him with their dark backs to him. He felt like he was rushing down a dark tunnel.

By the time they reached the living room, his mind was reeling. He saw, almost simultaneously, spilled drinks, mumbling islands of conversations, empty plates, overturned ashtrays, misplaced articles of clothing, wadded napkins, the half-lit dining room and nameless flaccid faces. He followed Stuart and Judith to the front closet. He saw Stuart put on his coat clumsily. He watched him hand Judith her coat without looking at her.

A cottony numbness seemed to ebb through his mouth and limbs. His parents were standing next to them and saying goodbye. Judith said something to his mother. He heard Stuart say thickly, "Great party—my lawyer'll have that rum condemned to public use if we don't make it home in one piece." Christopher's parents laughed and turned away toward another couple. Stuart fumbled with the door, then walked out while Judith put on her coat.

Judith looked up and saw Christopher watching her leave. He saw her dark eyes widen and her lips smile. His parents and the rest of the party seemed suspended in another dimension. Judith walked over to him through the half-lit continuum slowly and deliberately, and, as if not caring who saw them, closed her eyes and kissed him full on the lips. Before he could speak or move, she was out the door and running up the walk to her husband. For a few moments, Christopher saw her kiss him again and again, each time from a different direction, focusing first on her lips, then on the skin of her cheeks, then her hands on his face and again the kiss from every other possible direction. When he had visualized all the possibilities, he found himself standing silently at the door, watching her yellow coat disappear in the dreamy darkness, yet feeling so close to her that her presence eclipsed the fact of distance and every other sensation he felt.

Last Call

TOM let the phone ring one more time then set the receiver into its cradle. The receiver bumped against one of the cradle's prongs and fell onto his desk. He stared at it a few seconds, then knocked it on the floor.

"Goddamn it, Liz—where the hell are you?" he shouted.

The phone started beeping. Its metallic alarm echoed off the walls of the dorm. Tom shook his head and sat on his bed, leaving the phone where it was.

He stared at some pieces of tape sticking to the walls where his posters and photographs had been. He tried to imagine what the walls had looked like with the pictures on them but was forgetting already. He remembered how he had disliked the bland blue paint and the pebbly surface of the concrete blocks when he had moved in. And he remembered covering the walls with anything from magazine articles to girl's underwear. "The home is the reflection of the soul," his grandmother had said. He smiled as he remembered the giggling fits he and Liz had when they taped a pair of her panties to the corner above his bed. He brushed his hair back with his fingers and glanced over at the telephone.

He was about to give in and put it back in its cradle when the door slammed into the wall. A short, muscular young man walked in. He had a bag of groceries in one hand and a large suitcase in the other. Tom looked up and saw it was his friend, Jon, then continued staring at the telephone.

"Hey, Cisco," Jon said. He tossed his suitcase and groceries on Tom's couch.

Tom's face was drawn. "Hey, Jono. What's up?"

"Nothing—absolutely, irrevocably nothing. This place is like a goddamn morgue."

"School's out and all the little kiddies have gone home to play."

"Uh-huh."

Jon sat down on the couch. He spread his arms out along its back and propped one foot up on the opposite knee. Tom watched him as he looked out the window into the dorm's courtyard. How many bars had they been thrown out of this year? He could not remember. He got them mixed up with the frat parties and sorority nocturnals. Enough, he thought, more than enough. He wondered if Jon ever changed clothes—he always wore blue jeans, a faded baseball jersey, and clodhoppers.

"Jono—do you ever change your clothes?"

Jon turned to Tom with a sneer on his face, then looked back into the courtyard. After a few seconds, Jon jerked his head to the side and raised an eyebrow. He glanced quickly around the room and smirked when he saw the telephone.

"You know, your phone's off the hook, Cisco."

Tom looked at it and shrugged. "Yeah, so?"

"Just thought you might like to know."

"Thanks."

Jon smiled. "I don't see what you see in that wench, Cisco."

"What wench, Pancho?"

"The flat-chested wench that didn't answer the phone 'cause she skipped town without saying goodbye, Cisco."

"She didn't skip town—she's staying here over the summer. And she's not flat-chested."

"She *is* flat-chested, and if she didn't skip town, where the hell is she?"

"What the hell does it matter if she's flat-chested or not?"

Jon started to answer, but Tom interrupted him. "I know —you'll screw anything with big boobs. Boobs for the boob. They ought to have a TV show for you—Boobing for Dollars or You Bet Your Boobs or Boobs or Consequences. How the hell should I know where she is—you think I'm psychic?"

"I think it's a manifestation of your latent homosexuality. You like her trim, boyish figure as a sublimated substitute— admit it, Cisco, you love me." Jon batted his eyes and blew Tom a kiss.

"Quit trying to cheer me up, Pancho. You're depressing me."

Jon laughed and pulled the grocery bag onto his lap. "Ya wanna beer?"

"Maybe—what's it to you?"

"Nuthin." Jon reached into the grocery bag. "I was just gonna have one myself and thought maybe you might like to guzzle a few suds wid me, ya know what I mean, Cisco?" he said, imitating the dialect of a street hood.

"Yeah, Pancho." Tom smiled and reached for the beer Jon was holding out for him. It was barely past 9 a.m. and they were drinking again. Tom picked the telephone up and put it back in its cradle, shaking his head as he dropped it into place.

"You know, Jono, I think I'm going crazy."

"Hell, I've been trying to tell you that all year."

"Yeah, but—" Tom rubbed his eyes and shook his head. His hair was matted and lumpy. He looked around the room. The bookshelves were empty. There were no clothes lying about; he had packed them the night before. The maids had woken him up to strip the bed. The trash can was stuffed with the posters and photographs. The only other traces of his presence were the flute case and metronome on his desk and his shaving cream, razor and towel by the sink beneath the mirror. He had thought he might kill some time with the flute until it was time to go.

"Why won't Liz answer the phone? More pointedly, why do I care if Liz won't answer the phone?"

"That's probably what everyone within a half mile of here is wondering."

Tom winced. "Was I that loud?"

Jon nodded as he guzzled down the remains of his first beer.

"Well, you see what I mean?"

Jon crumpled the can in his fist and threw it at the trash can. It bounced off the trash and landed on the floor.

"Nope. I figured you were just drumming up one last gust of excitement before the summer doldrums hit." Jon grabbed another beer and pulled the ring-top off of it.

"I was sort of hoping she'd let me move in with her this summer."

"You? With Elizabeth? Are you crazy?"

"She's got her own apartment, and I could help her with the rent. And she likes my fluting."

"Yeah, but you're missing the point, Cisco. Liz is a stuck up little string bean that thinks we're a bunch of animals. And that's aside from the fact that the chick's lost in space, a lunar module heading for Uranus with all this ESP crap—you know what she said to me yesterday? "Your vibes are scrambling my astral projection—buzz off.""

Tom smiled. "Clever little wench, ain't she?"

"Yeah, but not for you."

Tom finished his beer and threw it at the trash can. It also bounced off the trash and landed on the floor. Jon handed him another beer, but before Tom opened it, he grabbed the metronome off the desk. He slipped its cover off, wound it up, and set it ticking. He watched the hypnotic swing of the arm back and forth.

"I might be losing my scholarship."

"Why? The dean find out you were screwing his secretary?"

Tom set the metronome down on his desk and in one fluid motion, grabbed the beer and pulled its ring top off. "No, that was a long time ago. Townsend—" The beer hissed and spewed foam over his hand. He quickly raised the can to his mouth and sucked up the foam. "—says I've reached my limit, she can't teach me anymore."

He raised his voice into a hostile whine. ""You play Bach like it's a mathematical puzzle—everything is perfect and on the beat and you think you've got it all. You're an arrogant smart aleck that misses the emotion, the feeling, the intuition of music." Tom sighed. "Then she went on about not expressing myself, playing like a metronome, bla, bla, bla. Stuff about right brains and left brains. She said I had a lot of thinking to do before she'd accept me as a student next year—the implication being, of course, *learn to play my way or you can screw your scholarship.*"

"What an asshole," Jon said. "Can she do that?"

"Yep. She holds the purse strings—she's the head of the review board."

"What are you going to do?"

"I dunno. It's sorta one of the reasons I wanted to talk Liz into letting me stay at her place over the summer, aside from other, more conspicuous advantages."

Jon sneered and rapidly flicked his tongue over his lips. Tom rolled his eyes.

"She might be a good influence on me."

"That'll be the day."

"Yeah, I guess so . . . She's mad at me about something and I haven't been able to sort it out." He took a long swig of his beer and stood up. "She quit talking to me since we all got thrown out of the White Stallion the other night."

Jon snorted. "Yeah, well, I think she's got a legitimate bitch there, Cisco."

"We just got drunk—"

"No, we didn't just get drunk—we got polluted. We were working on our sixth or seventh pitcher when you stood up and started auctioning off that pair of Liz's panties you had stuck up on your wall." Jon posed, holding his beer up in the air. "'Hear ye, hear ye, hear ye. The auction is about to proceed.' You were standing on your chair spilling beer on the guy behind you—that's how we got thrown out. 'What am I bid for a pair of dainty undies that but recently brushed the soft down of this lovely young wench's privates?'"

Tom walked in front of his mirror and looked at himself. "Did I say that?"

"Yes sir, Mr. Cisco. You may not remember 'cause the guy behind you knocked you off the chair, whereupon various and sundry drinks were distributed randomly about the room. Then two big bruisers grabbed you by the scruff of the neck and escorted our party out of doors."

"Hmph." Tom ran his hand along his chin. feeling his whiskers. "Yeah, I remember. So you think she's mad about that?"

"Well, then we were walking across the parking lot and you got down on all fours and vomited on somebody's right rear tire."

"I puked on somebody's car?" Tom bent over and turned the hot water on in his sink.

"Yeah—don't you remember? That's why we were running across the street when the police tried to pick us up for jaywalking—that car was full of friendly natives and they were chasing us. You evidently puked on some jerk's custom spoked wheels. He was going to make you lick it off."

Tom's eyes met the reflection of his eyes in the mirror. They looked sadder than the rest of his face. He stared at them while he spoke. "I remember getting chased, but I thought it was the guys in the bar."

He looked down and tested the water a couple of times, adjusted the cold and hot taps, then stuck his hands under the steaming faucet, wincing as the water gushed over his fingers and palms. He looked back up to his eyes in the mirror. They were bloodshot and had dark rings under them. "We got away, though, right?"

"Boy, for a musician you have one lousy memory, Cisco. You don't remember what happened when they were frisking you?"

Tom splashed some water on his face. "What were they frisking me for?"

"Drugs. You were thanking them for saving our lives from the friendly natives who got scared by the police siren. You were trying to shake their hands and give 'em tips—when you reached in your pocket, they racked you up against the car and started frisking you."

"Yeah, but I wasn't packing, so they had to let me go." Tom smiled at himself in the mirror and splashed some more water on his face.

"Well, except that when the cop that was frisking you got down around your knees—" Tom squirted a ball of shaving cream into his hand — "you broke wind in his face."

Tom looked at himself in the mirror and winced.

"I farted in the cop's *face*?"

Jon scooted over to the edge of the couch nearest the sink. "We, the genteel, refer to it as breaking wind, or perhaps crepitating, and refrain from such vulgar appellations of natural physiological functions."

Tom smeared the shaving cream over his face and rubbed it in. "You know, Pancho, I hate musicians."

Jon finished his second beer, crumpled the can and threw it at the corner, not even trying to hit the waste can. It bounced off the wall and rattled on the floor for a few seconds.

"Yeah, so?"

Tom flipped the cold water tap off and stuck his razor under the stream of hot water.

"I mean I *hate* 'em. I can't even stand to be around 'em." He gingerly touched the razor to his throat. He shaved slowly, as if he were nursing a dull blade through one last shave.

"Yeah, but Cisco—you *are* a musician. Remember your flute—all those recorders, your metronome, Townsend, scholarships?" Jon glanced over at the metronome ticking on the desk and opened a third can of beer. "Speaking of metronomes, do we have to have that thing ticking like a goddamn time bomb during our last tete-a-tete of the year?"

Tom stopped mid-stroke on the right side of his throat and pointed the razor at Jon.

"I tell you Pancho, they're sexually frustrated, nitpicking pedants that can't enjoy Mozart's Jupiter symphony—no, it has to be Scarlatti's Concerto #31 in D flat minor for flute and xylophone, published posthumously after having been found between the mattresses of his mistress's bed, stained with Scarlatti's precious genital fluids. And then it can't be any old recording of it they'll have—" He accidentally flipped some whiskered foam onto the floor. He ignored it, turning back to the mirror and sticking the razor under the water. "They'll have every recording of it and proceed to compare the listless quality of Isaac Tampax to the more sexually suggestive xylophoning of Carmen Suxcok. I hate 'em, Pancho—goddamn hate every one of 'em."

He finished with his throat and began delicately maneuvering the razor over his chin. His chin was square, but the dimple in the middle made it a particularly difficult section to shave. He pulled the skin of the left side of his chin up with his free hand and gave it a scrape. A trickle of blood flowed over his Adam's apple.

"Oops," he said.

Jon got up and stopped the metronome from ticking. "Teach you to shave while you're polluted, Cisco."

"I'm not polluted and I'm not just shaving, Pancho. You're witnessing the transubstantiation of gross flesh into angelic ether. You're watching the mystical cleansing of a soul, the redemption of an abject sinner in a bath of blessed holy water. This is a sacred rite for the eyes of initiates only." He tapped the razor on the edge of the sink and looked at his eyes in the mirror again.

Jon reached into the grocery bag and pulled out a pack of Kools. Ripping the pack open, he said, "You're going to need a lot of transubstantiating to get back into Liz's pants again." He stuck a cigarette in his mouth and lit it. "You know, she talked the police out of arresting you, Cisco."

Tom paused, then his shaving hand collapsed to his side and he shook his head at himself in the mirror. Several seconds lapsed. "Pancho, I . . . I really fucked up, didn't I?"

Jon nodded. "Yeah, I guess you could say that."

"She's a real sweetheart. A little on the dingy side, but a swell kid."

Jon smirked at Tom's half shaven face. Blood was dripping down his throat. His eyes were pained and serious while one cheek was puffed out with a thick layer of shaving cream and the other streaked with stray foam.

"Dingy, yes. But sweetheart? Don't get maudlin on me—you look like a clown." Tom turned abruptly to the mirror and heated up the razor. Jon took a couple of drags off his cigarette. "Don't you remember anything else that happened that night?"

The razor was clean, but Tom continued holding it under the hot water. He tapped it against the sink a couple of times, then turned to Jon. "I remember I walked over to her place, picked her up, and we walked down to the White Stallion and met you. We were having a good time. She was laughing a lot. We got pretty smashed, I got knocked over and spilled a few drinks. We got thrown out and some guys started chasing us. The police scared them off and we went home. Liz was a little pissed off."

Jon took a long drag off his cigarette and blew out a smoke ring that drifted across the room. "You have a conveniently selective memory, Cisco." Tom turned his back to him and began shaving again. "The cop you were uncouth to got ready to smack you with his billy club, but the other guy stopped him. Liz *pleaded* with them to let you go. She did everything but get down on her knees and do it right. You were still giggling and making an ass out of yourself. They wanted to take you in on a drunk and disorderly—let you cool off in the slammer. The guy with the offended nose wanted to stick you with resisting arrest." Tom continued shaving as if he were not listening. "Liz, in one of her few rational moments, told 'em we just lived down the street, that we were on our way home. She talked them into following us to make sure we went straight home. They bought it, even while you persisted in trying to kiss her and feel her up. It was a goddamn miracle."

Jon stopped to guzzle down the remains of his beer, then dropped the cigarette into the can. A thin stream of smoke drifted out. He shook the can and the cigarette gave a short hiss. Tom finished off the remaining side of his face, tapped the razor on the sink and ran the blade under the hot water. He flipped on some cold water and splashed his face a couple of times, then dunked his head under the faucet.

Jon continued, "She let us into her place and made us stand by the door till the cops left. When they were out of sight, she walked up to us with the meanest, iciest glare I ever saw and said, 'By the grace of my good karma you two animals are not in jail. Now get your repulsive prickfaces out of here and don't ever come back—' She started shoving us out the door—'And I mean it—don't ever come back!' Then she slammed the door and turned out her lights."

Tom began rubbing a towel over his head and said, "Well, I guess that's why she's not answering her phone, eh, Pancho?"

Jon nodded.

Tom stared at his eyes in the mirror. They stared back at him unsympathetically. He shook his head slightly. He looked at Jon's reflection, then his, then Jon's again. "Well, fuck her if she can't take a joke."

"My sentiment exactly, Cisco." Jon lit another cigarette and watched Tom drying his hair. "When are you splitting, anyway?"

"Oh, I dunno—what time is it now?"

Jon glanced down at his watch. "Ten."

"My grandmother should be picking me up around eleven. Then we're going up to Michigan for a couple of days to stay with my aunt. Then, back down to Chicago, where she'll make one last-ditch effort to keep my parents from splitting up. The grand tour."

Tom combed his hair, buttoned his shirt and tucked it in. He looked at himself in the mirror. The cowlicks were gone. His face looked clean and handsome, though his eyes were still ringed and bloodshot. *That's okay*, he thought to himself, *she'll just think I've been studying too hard.* He put his face up close to the mirror, picked some matter out of the corner of his eyes, then said, "What about you, Pancho? When are you blowing this popstand?"

"I've got an eleven o'clock train to catch, so I guess I'd better get going soon." He looked into the grocery bag and pulled out the last beer.

Tom sat down on his bed across from Jon. "You got anything to eat in there?"

"Yeah." Jon grabbed a bag of pretzels and tossed them to Tom. Tom opened them, took a few, and tossed them back.

"Well, Cisco," Jon said, "I guess this is about it, ain't it?"

"Yeah," Tom said through a mouthful of pretzels. He picked up his unfinished beer and took a swig." How are you getting to the train station?"

"Walking."

Tom looked out the window a few seconds. "We had a lot of fun this year, didn't we, Pancho?"

"Yeah, I guess you could say that."

Tom stood up suddenly and raised his beer in the air. "I propose a toast!"

Jon stood up and raised his beer up to Tom's. "Fire away, Cisco."

"Here's to getting polluted and thrown out of bars!"

They tapped their cans together.

"Hear, hear!" They guzzled the beers down, gasped and threw the cans at the corner.

"Well, Cisco, I'm taking off," Jon said.

He picked up his suitcase and walked toward the door. Tom followed him. Jon turned and held out his hand. Tom grabbed it and shook it.

"See ya this fall—or maybe we can get together this summer, Cisco."

"Yeah, maybe—that's a good idea. See ya, Pancho."

Jon walked out the door. Tom followed him and watched him walk down the hall.

"Watch out for Los Federales, Pancho!"

"Don't eat any wooden burritos, Cisco!"

Tom went back in his room and shut the door. He stopped at the sink and wrapped his razor and shaving cream in the towel, then opened the closet and pulled out two suitcases, one heavier than the other. He opened the lighter one and stuffed the towel in it. He picked up his flute and metronome and stuffed them in next to his towel. Then he sat down at his desk and stared at the telephone. He started to reach for it, then stopped. He rubbed his forehead with his fingertips, took a deep breath, and with a quick motion, grabbed the phone. His fingers were cold and trembling as he dialed. He put the phone up to his ear.

He waited several seconds, then said, "Hello, Liz? Uh . . . this is . . . this is Tom. I . . . I just wanted to call and say I'm sorry. I'm sorry about the other night and uh . . . I'm sorry I was a prickface. My grandmother's coming in a few minutes to pick me up and I'll be leaving for the summer. So, this is goodbye, sorta—I'm sorry I've been . . . well, you know. But we had fun, didn't we? At least I'm not a hopelessly antiseptic musician, a block of wood in the school band. I'm not that, am I? Those guys are about as witty as a bottle of Listerine. My parents— well, my mother and grandmother always wanted . . . well, I guess it doesn't matter. Goodbye, Liz. Goodbye. Have a nice summer. 'Bye."

Tom dropped the receiver on the desk. It fell on the floor. He picked up his bags and walked out the door without shutting it. The phone was still ringing on the other end as he walked down the hall.

Round Trip

AFTER a couple of hours, the car seemed to drive itself. Tom held the steering wheel with two limp fingers and let the countryside unravel before him. It was flat and green and shimmered beneath the early afternoon sun. Cornfields merged into soybean fields, which merged with wheat fields, farm houses and crossroad towns. His grandmother had fallen asleep beside him and was curled into a pillow propped against her side of the car. The air was thick and hot. Tom had opened the windows on his side of the car, but Mrs. Caines had insisted on keeping hers closed. She did not want her hair messed when they arrived at Evelyn's.

Mirages glimmered on the distant pavement. Sometimes Tom concentrated on one's quavering reflection until it disappeared and another took its place. His back was damp and the warm air blew hard on his face. He glanced at his grandmother. There was a moist sheen on her forehead. She was smiling in her sleep. Her neatly curled hair still held its shape beneath the fine webbing of a hairnet.

Tom was glad she had fallen asleep. He was tired of fending off her questions and listening to her stories about his relatives that were really parables designed to steer him toward some model of behavior. She was a former guidance counselor for the Peoria school system who had studied too much Pavlov in graduate school.

"How's my number one grandson?" she had asked when she picked him up at the dorm. Her eyes were bright and piercing.

"Exhausted after a week's worth of finals and looking forward to a well-earned vacation," he lied. He looked down into her eyes while he spoke. It was a simple enough question, but he knew she used it as a probe. She was looking for his emotional response, where his eyes looked, how his breathing rate changed, the position of his shoulders, head and hands. She was a practical woman who acted on these bits of information. She would see the dark rings under his eyes and begin probing.

He'd set his bags down near the trunk of her car and given her a quick hug. Her clothes smelled of hairspray and lilac sachet.

"How's my number one grandmother?" he asked.

"Fine," Mrs. Caines said. She smiled and looked him over. "Just fine. And proud to have such a handsome grandson."

Tom raised an eyebrow and through the side of his mouth said, "Watch it, Grandma, you're stepping on my Oedipus complex."

She laughed and the penetrating glint in her eyes disappeared. She gave him the keys to her old Plymouth.

"I'm the navigator this trip," she said as she got in the passenger side. "You're driving."

Tom threw his bags in the trunk. Mrs. Caines briskly opened a map of Illinois on her lap. The way to Albion, Michigan was traced in red ink. She slipped on a pair of black horn-rimmed glasses and ran her finger along the red line. Tom started the car.

"Pick up 57 outside of Champaign. We'll take that up to the 80 and bypass Chicago. We'll have about another hundred miles from there till we meet state highway 40." She snapped her glasses off and folded the map. "That should keep you busy for a while."

"Yes, ma'am!" he said. "Doesn't she get lonely living up there all by herself?"

"No—hardly." She rolled her eyes and pointed to a road sign. "You want to pick up the 57 North here . . . no, I've done the best I could to talk some sense into that girl, but she just won't leave the place. She's going to die an old maid. She could have an accident or get snowed in—it's dangerous." Mrs. Caines straightened her skirt. Its material rasped stiffly against her slip and nylons. "But she says she's happy. If I didn't go up there myself, I'd probably never see her . . ." Her voice trailed off for a few seconds as she looked around the seat for her purse. She found it beneath her feet. "You'll be able to rest there before the fireworks begin at your parents'."

For the next hour Tom had been on guard as she asked about his reaction to his parents' separating, how school was going, and why he looked so tired. He did not tell her. He had managed to keep her talking until the rhythmic thumping of the highway's seams and the stifling heat lulled her to sleep.

Tom's attention focused on a mirage again. He wondered if he would actually think it was water if he were dying of thirst. He doubted it. The longer his grandmother was asleep the freer his thoughts became. Earlier his mind had felt like a tightly wound spring about to snap loose. Every time he relaxed his grip, a weak feeling would ebb through him and images of his parents not wanting him to come home, or his girlfriend Liz not answering the phone, or his professor threatening to eject him from the music department, would whirl by.

He had made a little game out of assigning different worries to the various fields he passed. He pretended they were like reels of film falling out of the trunk and rolling off the highway. A series of cornfields became the dump yard for his grades. A recently manured soybean field became the dump yard for the trouble he was having with the head of the music department. A fallowing field became Elizabeth's dumping him. He watched them shrink in the rear view mirror until they disappeared, then he would select another problem and dump it. He felt like a cross between Johnny Appleseed and a chemical waste disposal unit. Each time one disappeared he would shrug and mutter, "Hmph."

It got hillier as they approached Chicago, and the mirages stopped. The occasional island of white clouds had gradually clumped together into lumpy masses of blue and gray. He was complacently enjoying the cooler, earthy-smelling air. He distinguished the aromas of soybeans, wheat, corn, and hay. As he rounded the top of a hill, a vast, shadowed plain spread out before him. Different shades of green formed a living patchwork quilt that stretched as far as he could see. Two or three shafts of sunlight broke through the layered clouds like celestial fingers touching the ground. Tom stared at them until they disappeared in the rear-view mirror.

His grandmother woke up soon after that. Their even-paced cruising had been interrupted by Tom's having to slow down and speed up to weave in and out of pockets of traffic. It was a little past two as they entered the outskirts of Chicago. Mrs. Caines pulled the map out of the glove compartment.

"Well, I guess it's about time for me to be the navigator again, isn't it?"

Tom glanced at her and nodded. Her face was puffy and wrinkled on the side she had been sleeping on.

"When you get to 80, take it northeast." Tom nodded again.

"Then, after about a hundred miles, we should run into state highway 40 and that'll take us up to Albion. Evie lives another twenty miles from there."

"Then we should get there around five," Tom said.

"More like six. We should pull over and call her."

"Okay." Tom felt more lighthearted than before, but he still did not feel like talking. Her being awake somehow changed the free-spirited mood he had been in; he felt on guard and introverted again.

Gary, Indiana seemed like an endless series of smokestacks billowing yellow or blue smoke. They stopped outside Gary to warn Evelyn of their imminent arrival. For a while it seemed to Tom that they were caught in an immense sym-metrical traffic formation evacuating the cities, but around Marcellus the traffic abruptly disappeared. The clouds had broken up a little, somewhere outside of Gary, and the air had gotten hot again. Tom had subliminally assumed things would cool off the further north they went, but that didn't happen until around five, when they were outside Albion. There the land flattened for a while and the state highway stretched into a long, dreamy V that seemed to disappear below the horizon.

From there, the roads got narrower and more deserted. The closer they got to Evelyn's house, the fewer crossroads towns they saw. There were several unattended farms; the countryside looked like a rambling garden tended by an open-minded, invisible gardener.

They drove up an incline for about half a mile, and as they reached the top of the hill, they saw Evie standing at her mailbox waving to them. A cluster of pale yellow cabbage butterflies twirled over her head. She was wearing a white sundress and sandals. She looked too vulnerable to be living on her own. The driveway tunneled through a thick stand of pine trees, at the center of which was her house. Evie ran up to the car and opened the door for Mrs. Caines. She pulled her out and gave her a hug and asked about their trip. The two of them took off chatting and seemed to have forgotten Tom altogether. He watched them patiently from the other side of the car.

Up close, Evie looked less fragile. Her hair and eyes were brown, her skin ruddy, and her lips pale. She wore no makeup and looked to be in her late thirties. Tom watched her next to his grandmother. They were both 5'8", but Evie looked shorter in her sandals. He could see the family resemblance in their full lips, long foreheads and square, dimpled chins. Evie was not pretty, but there was an earthy attractiveness to her that Tom liked immediately. She looked up abruptly and smiled.

"Hi, Evie," Tom said across the top of the car.

"I don't believe it!" Evie said. She shook her head and stared at him a few seconds. "Are you the same little brat I used to tease?"

Tom shrugged sheepishly and nodded. He'd forgotten it had been that long.

"Well, come here and let me take a look at you," she beckoned with both hands. "Come on, don't be shy!"

Tom walked around the car. Evie promptly kissed him on the cheek.

"Welcome, cuz—or is it neph? I get mixed up figuring out my relation to your side of the family."

"You're second cousins," Mrs. Caines said.

"Well, anyways, welcome. Let's get your things inside so you two can relax. I made some iced tea—"

"With orange juice and mint?" Mrs. Caines asked.

"Precisely according to your recipe."

"Now aren't you the bee's knees."

They walked together toward the house. Tom followed with the bags. The air was pervaded by the scent of pines; the driveway wore a thick blanket of rust-colored pine needles. Evie's house was set on the exact top of the hill. Its redwood siding and the surrounding trees almost hid it from view.

"This weather is absolutely muggy and I apologize for it," Evie said as they entered the house.

"That's fine," Mrs. Caines said. "It's not your fault. You weren't waiting out there for us, were you?"

"Oh, no! I mean, not for long. I heard the car coming. You get so you can hear any engine within a half mile of here."

She led them to the back of the house, telling them the walls were rough-sawn cedar and that was why the house smelled of cedar. She turned to Tom. "This is your grandmother's room. Yours is on the first floor."

Tom set Mrs. Caines' bags down in her room, then went down to his room. Evie followed him in.

"You can see the swamp from here," she said. She pulled the drapes open. Tom set his suitcase on a chair and opened it, then walked over to the window. "It's not actually a swamp," Evie continued, "it's a marsh. It's a depression in the land left by retreating glaciers. There used to be a lot of marshes up here, but most of them have been drained."

"It looks like a swamp to me."

"It's not. Its plant life is predominantly various species of grasses—swamps have trees."

Mrs. Caines walked in. "Evie, where's that iced tea you were bragging about?"

"Oh!" Evie ran out of the room and up the stairs. "I'm sorry—I forgot. Come on up to the living room—it's all ready."

Tom and his grandmother joined her and sat down next to floor-to-ceiling windows overlooking a porch. They were on the top floor of the house and the porch was surrounded by the tops of the pine trees. A series of birds were flying on and off the porch's bird feeder. Tom walked up to the windows and peered into the trees.

"This is like living in a treehouse," he said.

"That's actually the way I planned it." Evie handed Mrs. Caines her iced tea and brought a glass to Tom. "I wanted the west side to face into the treetops and the north side to have a view of the marsh." Tom watched the birds systematically dart onto the porch railing, jump on the feeder as soon as another left, then fly back to the dense foliage of the pine trees. It was a pattern that repeated itself over and over with different birds. "They have a strict pecking order," Evie said. "Blue jays, titmice, nuthatch, chickadees, then cardinals. That's a chickadee there now. Then they have their pecking order within their species. The big, aggressive ones feed first and so on. I somehow managed to land my house right in the middle of a bird lane, so there's a constant stream of birds at dawn and dusk."

"You've done quite well with your inheritance," Mrs. Caines said. She remained seated, watching the two of them framed by the picture window. "I'm sure your father would be quite proud."

Evie continued staring out the window at the flow of birds. Tom saw her look down. He became conscious of his hands and the beads of moisture clinging to his glass, then noticed he was standing almost shoulder-to-shoulder with her. He felt awkward and naked under his grandmother's gaze and moved away to sit back down in his chair.

Evie swung around and Tom's body tensed.

"How's your iced tea, Aunt Lillian?" she asked abruptly.

Mrs. Caines glanced at Tom and smiled. It was the feline smile of a therapist playing cat and mouse with an irrational patient.

"I couldn't have made it better myself, Evie," she said. Her eyes were amused and attentive. "I couldn't have made it better myself."

"Well, that's fine," Evie said. "I'm glad you like it."

Tom noticed that the sun was dipping below the tree tops. Evie's white dress gleamed with the reflection of the yellow light. Her eyes were dark and impenetrable. She suddenly grabbed Tom's hand.

"Dinner will be ready in half an hour and I know you're absolutely dying to see my marsh and all my toads and frogs, so if you want to get a good look at it today, you have to go down now before the mosquitoes break loose." Tom was so surprised by her lightheartedness that he did not know what to say. She whisked him from his chair and said over her shoulder, "We'll be back in time for dinner, Aunt Lillian—and we promise not to talk to strangers."

Mrs. Caines stared at her lap. Then she straightened her skirt and smiled. "Well, just make sure you don't track any mud back into the house or you'll get a spanking for dessert."

"Yes, ma'am," Evie shouted, nudging Tom through the door, "We'll be careful."

As soon as Evie had shut the door behind them, Tom's feeling of skittishness went away. Evie stood on the landing, leaning against the railing, gazing at the marsh. Tom stopped a few steps below her. Countless birds were chattering loudly, like an aviary audience waiting for a show to start.

"Are you all right?" he asked.

Evie turned her gaze into his upturned face.

"Lovely. Absolutely lovely." She ran her hand along the railing and started down the steps. "No, I'm fine. I just don't think I'll ever convince her how happy I am here."

"She didn't seem particularly disappointed—"

Evie stopped abruptly and said, "You don't have to play diplomat with me." Tom looked up to her dark eyes. "You know as well as I that was the opening salvo to a barrage of inexorable logic leading to Chicago, two kids, two cars, a husband, and dinner at six. She's determined to get some grandnephews out of me yet."

Evie reached out and thumped Tom on the forehead. "She does the same thing with you, only she uses your mother instead of your father, hopeless Freudian that she is." Tom's face flushed. Evie came down to the step he was on and rested her hand on his shoulder. "Doesn't she?"

Tom turned away without answering and continued down the steps. She was right. He knew she was right, but something kept him from admitting it. At the bottom of the steps, two small toads, no more than an inch long, jumped out of his way. Tom saw them just in time to avoid stepping on them. He suppressed an urge to bend over and sweep them up in his hand. He looked at Evie, who was smiling as if she knew what he had almost done.

"Bufo Americana."

"Huh?"

"The toads. Cute little buggers, aren't they?"

Tom nodded yes. The birds continued chattering as if he and Evie were not there. They stood in the dark shadow of the house cast by the setting sun, staring at each other.

"Don't you think you're being a little presumptuous about her?"

Evie stepped past him to a path tunneling through thigh-high grasses and weeds that led to the marsh.

"Do you?" she asked.

"All she said was that your father would be proud of you. That sounded pretty tame to me." Evie started down the path, brushing the tops of the grasses with her hands. Tom followed her.

"Yeah, but that's not what Lillian meant," she said over her shoulder. "She thinks I'm crazy to live up here without a husband—it's not natural."

Tom started to ask her how sensible it was to live so far out by herself, but something stirred in the bushes off the side of the path. He froze. It sounded like a snake. His eyes darted around his feet, trying to penetrate the dense plant growth. Evie continued ahead of him. He could hear leaves rustling a few feet ahead of him. He wished he had worn boots, then noticed the thick buzzing of hundreds of insect wings. The bushes the noise came from rustled again. It was a small thicket of blackberries. Hovering about it were honey bees, large metallic blue flies, swarms of gnats and brown-spotted deer flies. The rustling stopped. A praying mantis the size of a small bird stood poised above a cluster of blackberry blossoms, a large brown moth twitching in its pincers. Tom laughed at himself and ran to catch up with Evie. Her head, shoulders, and waist were drifting above the yellow tassels of wild grass. She was still talking as if he were just behind her.

"— her neatly arranged psychological boxes, then it's not right. They're like a cement labyrinth around her psyche." She stopped and turned around to face Tom. "You can feel it, can't you—the dynamic excess of life? This whole meadow is charged with life."

Tom heard the humming insect wings, the muffled rasp of leaves brushing against each other, the background chattering of birds up at the house. He nodded yes.

Evie continued, "I've gotten so I can feel the plants and trees growing—I can sense the roots pressing through the soil and leaves stretching to consume more and more light." She darted off the path and jerked a black-eyed Susan's blossom into her hand. "Look at this—this is condensed light." She held the bright yellow flower in front of him, its petals trembling in her grasp. "Condensed light, don't you see? All it is is light and dirt. Eight minutes ago, the light you're seeing this with was on the surface of the sun. A few million years ago a hydrogen atom fused with another hydrogen atom and this stuff, this light right here on this flower and my hand and your eyes, radiated through the layers of the sun to arrive here. It's a damn miracle unfolding right in front of us—and you just don't see it happening in Chicago. You just don't see it."

The path ended abruptly in front of them and spread into the muddy outer regions of the marsh. There was a faint odor of decay that had become stronger as they reached the edge of the stagnant water. Flat green pads of water lilies floated on its brown surface. Tom heard a series of plops and splashes as unseen frogs jumped in. A couple of small, red-winged blackbirds flew out of a patch of cattails off to the right of Evie. Evie held her finger to her lips and pointed to a dense section of olive and brown sedges. Tom did not see anything and shrugged. Evie kept pointing and Tom saw a large, squat, camouflaged bird standing like a brown bowling pin with its beak pointed straight up in the air.

"American bittern," Evie whispered. "Clever little twit, isn't he?"

"Yeah," Tom whispered back, but too loudly—the bittern jumped and flew off with a noisy flapping of its outstretched wings.

"Oh well," Evie said aloud. "This is the marsh. Did you know I had an M.S. in earth science?"

Tom shook his head and said, "No."

"Well, I do and this is my living laboratory."

Tom smacked his forearm. Two bloody mosquitoes were stuck to his palm. "I think you've got a little too much life buzzing around here."

"Yeah, maybe. We should start heading back before the rest of the swarms find out we're here." Evie picked up a stone imbedded in the dirt. "You see this?" She showed the stone to

Tom. It had sparkly, metallic flecks in it, but was an otherwise unnoteworthy rock.

"A brown rock with fool's gold in it." Tom stepped ahead of her. Something about her persistence annoyed him.

"Iron pyrite," she said to his back. "Somewhere between five and ten billion years ago, in some aging corner of the galaxy, a star blew up and fused a bunch of helium and maybe carbon together. Somewhere clear on the other side of the galaxy, maybe. The only way heavy atoms like iron can be created is in the tremendous heat of a supernova. Some plant will suck some of it up and it eventually becomes hemoglobin. It's kind of like reincarnation."

Tom brushed away more and more mosquitoes. The sun was below the horizon and seemed to be dragging a blanket of flat, flame-colored clouds off the edge of the earth. The path was dark. A few frogs started croaking. The air was still warm and muggy. Beads of sweat trickled down Tom's face.

"It seems to me," Tom said, his eyes focused on the house, "you could have the same awareness of these things without having to live like a hermit."

Evie stopped mid-step. one of her hands fell limply to her side. She looked at the rock in her other hand, then at Tom walking back toward the house. The rock slipped out of her fingers and fell into the darkness around her feet.

"You try it and see how it goes," she whispered.

When he did not hear an answer, Tom decided to drop the subject. He arrived at the steps with the fading light of dusk barely reaching through the trees. The birds were quiet, but he could hear the voices of a large chorus of croaking frogs from the marsh. Evie followed Tom up the steps, trailing her hand along the railing. Mrs. Caines was waiting for them at the door.

"Did you have a nice walk?" she asked.

Tom wrapped his arm around his grand-mother's waist. "Yeah!" He wrinkled his face. "Except for the mosquitoes. I thought I heard a snake, too."

"No!" Mrs. Caines clucked her tongue.

Evie quietly shut the door behind her and went into the kitchen. Mrs. Caines led Tom into the dining room, listening to his story about the snake and the praying mantis.

Dinner passed quickly. After a couple of glasses of wine, Tom felt full and lighthearted. Mrs. Caines steered the conversation towards relatives' families, marriages, and children whenever possible. Tom exaggerated drinking escapades at school. Evie listened. Her attention seemed to wander toward the windows facing the marsh unless Tom spoke directly to her.

They went to bed soon after that. Tom was tired and ached to sleep. He opened the bedroom windows and checked the screen to make sure no mosquitoes could get in. Sitting on the end of the bed, he tried to see the marsh, but the cloud cover had cut off whatever starlight or moonlight there was, and beyond the limit of the bedroom lamp's light there was an eerie darkness out of which frogs' voices echoed up the hill. Some heat lightning illuminated the clouds, but not enough that he could see anything distinctly. Tom turned off the lamp and pulled the sheets over his shoulders. The absolute darkness disturbed him. He waved his hand in front of his face but could not see anything, not even a blur of motion. It was a little scary to him and he had trouble falling asleep despite the weight of tiredness he felt. He kept expecting something to reach out and grab him. He reasoned to himself that there was nothing to be scared of and wearily forced his thoughts onto reviewing what had been an unusually long day. He fell asleep thinking of the mirages he had seen shimmering on the flat, hot pavement.

His sleep was disturbed by a series of unpleasant dreams. He dreamt of school and Elizabeth and his parents. He dreamt he was at an audition, but his flute was heavy and responding slowly. A metronome kept speeding up and slowing down while a faceless audience wiggled and fidgeted with a fluid, frenetic energy to a mysterious, animated rhythm. They kept getting in and out of their seats and fanning themselves with their programs. He saw his grandmother and his music teacher frowning in the front row. The ticking metronome got louder and he tried to play over it. Elizabeth was standing in the aisle. Her blouse was unbuttoned. She was singing and thumping her fingers on her thighs to a rock beat. Someone began pounding on a set of drums, drowning out the rhythm of the metronome. Tom blew harder on the flute.

The drumming got louder. His grandmother and his music teacher started shouting. Tom tried to play over them, but he could not. Their voices were shrill and angry. His grandmother shouted at him. The teacher shouted at the metronome. He became frantic. The muscles of his face were aching. The drumming became wild and erratic, then something exploded in him and he threw the flute at the drums with all the power he had. The drumming stopped. The drummer stood up. It was Evie.

Tom's eyes jerked open. His heart was racing. The sheets were limp with sweat. Something was beating frantically on the window screen. Tom's mind screamed, but his mouth was clamped shut. The urge to leap out of bed swept over him. He found himself crouching by the door, shivering. His entire body was damp with sweat and his hands were shaking. The thrashing at the window filled his entire consciousness with a fear as large as the room. His hands clutched for something to protect himself with. His eyes were wrenched to the window.

A pale green moth the size of his hand was beating its wings against the aluminum mesh. Tom shuddered. It was just a moth. A big moth, he thought, but just a moth. Nothing. He laughed, pushing himself up with his back against the wall. He teased himself for being so scared. "Brother—you are one dumb motherfucker, Cisco," he said aloud. He laughed again.

He did not stop to think why he could see the moth or why it was thrashing at the window. He took two steps toward the screen and dropped to his knees. Nausea paralyzed him on the floor. There were three lights hovering outside the window.

"Oh Jesus," he moaned. His mouth was clammy. His arms and legs were weak. His chest was stiff and it felt like his heart was pounding against a solid wall. He was afraid they might hear it. "This can't be happening," he thought.

He crawled against the wall beside the window in case they had guns. Any second he expected a hand to burst through the window screen. The seconds passed with maddening silence. There were no frogs croaking or crickets chirping. The house was completely silent. He waited, but heard nothing. No sticks breaking beneath a heavy step, no voices, no sound at all. The moth had flown away from the window. He could see the silhouettes of the lamp, bed, suitcase and chair. A pale shaft of light shone through the window making an elongated rectangle on the wall. The lights had moved closer.

Tom could not wait any longer. *If it's going to happen, let it happen now*, he thought. He edged toward the window and peeked over the window sill. There were three intensely bright, blue-white balls of light suspended above the field about thirty feet from the house. They did not react to his head's appearing in the window. He sat up on his knees to get a better look.

Two of the lights appeared stationary. The third and largest one was moving slowly toward the house. The grasses and shrubs were cast in an odd, highly contrasted light that appeared to shift from absolute light to absolute darkness with no shades of gray in between. There was nothing holding the lights up.

It did not make sense, he thought. Lamps? No poles or bodies holding them up. Marsh gas? They weren't over the marsh. UFO's? No noise. A shiver went over him. Ghosts? He squinted at the largest ball. There was no face, just a globular cluster of light. It suddenly swept several feet closer. Tom ducked beneath the window. An electric terror ripped through his brain. The bluish glow grew brighter, the elongated rectangle of light passing through the window spread across the room like two arms sweeping open, a flood of phosphorescence pouring in between them.

Tom's efforts to frame it, to identify it and contain it in a category of something knowable disintegrated. His mind split. A feeling of dreamy spaciousness rushed through him and out of his body. Something in him merged with the phosphorescence. He stood up and faced the window. His body was bathed in light. A vast wave of heat lightning shimmered through the clouds. He heard a voice say "God, " and he fainted.

IT was a mockingbird that lured him to consciousness. It ran through its various calls, chirping like a sparrow, then a blackbird or chickadee, then whistling through a robin's call, then cawing like a crow. The bird's cheerful abandon coaxed him awake. He listened with his eyes closed, aware of nothing but the bird's various melodies and a peaceful, mental spaciousness.

He opened his eyes. The sun was up. He was huddled against the wall beneath the window. He was naked. His nakedness startled him and his hands rushed to pull some clothes on him before someone walked in the door. For a moment he wondered what he was doing on the floor, then he remembered. The stairs outside creaked. He heard someone coming down the steps. Tom jumped onto the bed and glanced out the window. The clouds had broken up. The hazy morning sunlight poured down on the marsh. It seemed to stick to all of his senses.

There was a knocking at the door.

"Tom?" It was Evie. "Breakfast's ready."

He stood up and called, "Evie?" He wanted to talk to her. He opened the door, but she had run back up the stairs. He ran his palm along the paneling, then leaned his face against the wood. He inhaled the cedar fragrance. He felt different. He went back in the room and stared at the marsh for a while, then decided to go on up for breakfast.

As he went up the stairs, he heard Evie's and his grandmother's voices.

"It's similar to the formation of mirages," he heard Evie say. "The air cools rapidly as it rises, but there are warm pockets above. The varying densities operate like sealed containers and the gas—" Tom inhaled sharply "—moves along a corridor of warm air, sandwiched between two denser layers. Eventually it breaks through and diffuses."

Mrs. Caines saw Tom enter the room.

"Well, look who's risen from the dead, Evie."

Evie turned to him. "Good morning, Tommie. Are you hungry?"

His face was pale and his eyes looked directly into hers.

"What were you just talking about?"

"Evie was telling me about the swamp gas."

Mrs. Caines was cheerful and seemed proud of Evie's understanding of natural phenomena. Tom's blood was pounding hard in his veins. He felt a griefy ache in his chest.

"It wasn't swamp gas," Evie said, "It was marsh gas."

Tom sat down next to Evie. "What was marsh gas?"

"Oh—some pockets of marsh gas made it up the hill last night and I was explaining how it happens to Aunt Lillian." Evie stood up. "Would you like some bacon and eggs?"

Tom looked up to her face plaintively. "They were marsh gas?"

"Hm-hmm." She went into the kitchen.

"Oh." He looked down at his feet. He felt like he was hurtling to earth. He stared at his bare feet.

"You look tired," his grandmother said.

He felt like a fool. His cheeks were burning and he wanted to disappear.

"I forgot my shoes," he said.

Evie returned with a steaming plate of scrambled eggs and bacon and set it on a tray near the porch facing the trees.

"Come and get it," she said. She watched him with a peculiar attentiveness.

Tom rose stiffly and sat in front of the tray. Mrs. Caines left the room. Tom started eating, but he did not taste anything. He felt deflated and ashamed. He winced at the thought that he had almost told Evie what had happened.

"You need to shave," Evie said.

Tom looked up as far as her pale lips. "I will," he answered. A tear blurred his vision and he looked away. Evie seemed to be waiting for him to say something. He looked at the bird feeder on the porch.

"Where are the birds?"

"They've already fed," Evie said.

"Oh." He continued eating, nudging fragments of scrambled eggs onto his fork with a piece of bacon.

"Are you all right?" Evie asked.

"Yeah, I'm fine," Tom said. "I feel much better now that I've eaten." His voice almost broke. He set his fork down and ate the remaining strip of bacon.

"Good." Evie took his plate and went into the kitchen.

Mrs. Caines returned and sat down with a map in her lap. She began tracing the way to Highland Park.

"When are we leaving?" Tom asked.

"In a couple of hours, after you get cleaned up and ready to go and I finish visiting with Evelyn."

Tom was glad. He could not wait to get away. He was glad they were leaving and he was glad he had not said anything to Evie.

"I'm doing my navigating," Mrs. Caines said.

Tom smiled. "That's good. You're good at it, Grandma. You do the navigating."

Tom avoided Evie the rest of the morning. He shaved and washed up. He put his shoes on and packed his suitcase. He sat on the edge of his bed and stared at the marsh. He felt normal and whole and was anxious to leave. When he ran out of things to do, he clipped his fingernails. Then he opened his suitcase and unpacked his metronome. He liked listening to its rhythmic ticking.

They left early that afternoon. Tom said goodbye to Evie and gave her a hug. She still seemed to be waiting for him to say something. She walked him and his grandmother out to the car and blew a kiss to them as they drove off.

Tom glanced in the rear-view mirror. He saw Evie standing beside her mailbox waving goodbye. He watched her figure shrink in the distance. At the bottom of the hill he asked Mrs. Caines which way to turn. A large green moth was twirling over Evie's head as they turned left onto the deserted highway.

David: Stung by
a Dead Bee

NORTH Green Street, being a main street, was a busy street except after the bars closed, well into the early hours of morning. Then, the last few students drifted home, singly or in pairs, stumbling past the uninhabited shops, only vaguely conscious of their whereabouts or direction. Some sang drinking songs and slapped each other on the back; others slipped in doors lit by yellow porch lights, perhaps still hoping to meet someone as the sound of the latch slipping into place carried through the listless night air.

The tenant that entered 1002 N. Green Street, David Kitt, lived in the back room on the first floor. Scents, both dusty and floral, hung in all the first floor rooms because his landlady kept several tropical plants along the front windows and insisted on keeping the windows shut for fear of the plants' catching a chill from the unpredictable Midwest weather. David's room, having once been the drawing room of an aging English professor who had entertained his friends and proteges there until he retired, retained an additional odor of tobacco which no amount of cleaning or incense could eliminate.

David entered the stuffy room quietly, slowly pulling the door shut behind him, though his senses still tingled with the ebbing exhilaration of nearly getting into a fight. He had stopped at The Way Inn on the way home from a movie. He had felt too intense and stimulated by the film to simply return to his empty, motionless apartment. He felt too warm and restless and wanted to prolong the vibrant sensation.

He had walked into the bar, extroverted and alert, trying to consume all the atmosphere at once. He absorbed the animated gestures and laughter; the pulsation of thick, heavy music; the subdued flashing lights; the aura of glee; the bartenders, waitresses, and beer. He smiled and sat in a booth by himself. Amidst all the commotion he felt placid and relaxed.

As he looked into his third glass of beer, he heard some shouting that included his name.

"Hey—Kitt!"

David looked around to see who was yelling for him.

"Kitt!" He heard again from behind. He looked over his shoulder and saw a group of students from school that ate at the same cafeteria he did—Jon Fox, Tom Caines and three or four others he recognized, but did not know their names.

"What?" David asked.

"Could you come over here and settle somethin'?" Jon asked.

David set his mug down and stood up, still slightly day-dreaming and not quite registering what was going on. He walked over to them, a little unsteady from the beers. They were slouched into their chairs beneath a haze of smoke, smirking while David approached.

"Settle what?"

"Why are you over there by yourself?" Jon asked.

"What?"

"What are you doing over there—jerking off?"

"Is that all you called me over for?" David started to go back to his table.

"No, no—wait a sec—we need you to settle a bet—you're an English major, aren't you?"

"Yeah—" David turned back around.

"Me too, but these uncivilized heathens won't believe me, so I need you to settle something."

"Cut it out, Jono," Tom said, shoving him in the ribs.

"Cut what out, Cisco?" Jon shoved him back. "I need his vote—"

"Leave him alone."

"We need to straighten this out once and for all and Kitt'll know for sure—so, Kitt, isn't Professor Wilson a fag?" Tom kicked Jon under the table and Jon elbowed him back.

"Why—are you looking for some action?" David asked.

"Are you offering?" Jon said, smiling to the other guys.

"No, but I am a little surprised—aren't you and Tom a couple?"

"Fuck you, you fudge packing fag." Tom pulled Jon back into his seat while one of the other guys started chanting, "Jonnie and Tommie sitting in a tree, k-i-s-s-i-n-g . . ."

Jon shouted, "Shut the fuck up, Mark!" and threw the contents of a bowl of nuts at him. Mark tried to dodge the debris, but was too drunk to do so without falling off his chair.

Tom stood up between Jon and David and pushed David in the chest. "Ignore these jerks— they don't know how to behave because they think God is dead—they can't help themselves."

David shoved Tom's hand off his chest, and Jon threw a mug of beer at them, shouting, "Cool these dogs off—they're in heat." The beer splashed across David's face and chest, and he looked for something to throw back, but Tom shoved him away from the table.

"Go on—just get out of here before someone does something really stupid."

"You go take care of your boyfriend, asshole," David said as he shoved Tom into Jon's lap. Tom laughed and put his arm around Jon, pretending to snuggle him into his chest.

"You mean like this?"

"Yeah, just like that." David shook his head and headed back to his table.

Instead of sitting down, he motioned to the waitress to bring him his check, which he paid, then left while Tom and his group of friends laughed over something David could not hear.

The brisk walk home erased most of the lingering thrill of potential danger. As he came up the walk to his building, he was becoming more aware of the feeling of poignant loneliness that had driven him out of his apartment to begin with. The stuffy apartment and the silence had aggravated the feeling to the point of being unbearable, and he'd had to leave.

Now, upon returning, he was struck again by the stale odors, but found himself peculiarly adjusted to them, having worked some of the restless loneliness out of his system. He left the lights off and sat in an old leather chair placed near a set of windows facing the backyard. He glanced around the cramped room.

Whether he liked it or not, he had to live there. His scholarship included the room as housing. It was moderately neat, aside from some scraps of paper strewn around the wastebasket and some clothes piled on a chair in the corner. He kept four or five books, each marked where he had left off, beside his bed. Among them were paperbound copies of *The Meaning of Art* by Sir Herbert Read, *Gnosis in the Christian Scriptures* by William Kingsland, and a very worn copy of Salinger's *Frannie and Zooey*. From his window he could see the shadows of a few honeysuckle bushes that formed a poorly defined hedge.

It was at the window that he did most of his reading and where he frequently wrote poetry. Something about the view gave him the impression he was an invisible witness to the pageant of life as the most dramatic seasonal changes passed before his gaze. He could stare out the window, lose track of time, and suddenly find himself sitting in the dark watching the last glimmer of sunlight fade from the horizon. Sometimes weeks would pass and he would sit down to find the summer had somehow imperceptibly passed into fall.

When the shorter days of fall came, dusk fell while David ate dinner. He rarely stayed in the cafeteria after eating, preferring wandering around the city to listening to one student's vain banter or another's futile arguments. The few times he remained, he was drawn inevitably into arguing with Tom Caines or one of his friends.

When David left the cafeteria, the houses outside had already grown silent. The sky above him had an iridescent deep blue of twilight, and towards it, the streetlights lifted their nebulous halos.

The crisp air distracted him, dispersing any motivation he had to study. The distant shouts of students playing football echoed in the silent street. His evening walks brought him through the dark tunnels of trees hanging over residential sidewalks, to the alleys behind the stores where rotting odors rose from the garbage cans, to the alcoves in the park where couples talked quietly and kissed, or musicians played for free. When he returned to his apartment, the light from the porch filled the path leading up to the steps. If the landlady was still there, he would stay on the porch smoking cigarettes until she left. Or, if the girl across the street had her window open, he would watch her from the shade of the veranda. He waited to see whether she would leave the light on or switch it off. If she turned it off, he would leave his shade and go in the house, resolved to catch up on his studies. If she left it on, he waited to see her figure highlighted by the lamp near the half-open window. Sometimes he mocked himself, but nevertheless sat on the porch looking at her. Her hair fell across her shoulders, and sometimes she would stare out her window as if she were looking straight at him.

Sometimes, in the morning, he waited at the window by the door pretending to arrange his books. The venetian blinds would be pulled so he could not be seen. When she came out, he would slip out to follow her. He would stay behind, keeping her figure in sight until their paths diverged as they reached the university buildings.

For no intelligent or justifiable reason, her image accompanied him through his classes and breaks. He walked through crowded halls, jostled by worried students and late professors, among pledges chanting ridiculous passages of Ionesco, past

solicitors handing out leaflets or selling underground newspapers and offering some patter about the inequities of the
government. These noises merged into one uniform sensation
for David, a sensation he treated as a test of his imaginary
devotion, which he kept safe and unrubbed by the hands of
foes. Her image sprang to his mind in poems and songs. He
was moody and sometimes overcome by an uncontrollable lan-
guor. He thought little of his future. He did not know whether
he would ever speak to her, or what he could say that would
keep him in her imagination, but he was constantly attuned
to any percept relaying her figure, her voice, her gestures—
anything. He was like a sentient radio sensitive only to her
transmissions.

This evening, although he felt a peculiar sense of pride from
the confrontation with Caines, as if he had unexpectedly ful-
filled some lingering, long-term desire, he was still not ready
to go to sleep. It was a dark, humid night, and there was no
sound in the house. Through his open window, he heard the
soft sounds of leaves brushing against each other. Some distant
light filtered through the gently swaying branches. He felt satisfied with seeing only the shaded forms of objects, as if ready
to slip into another dimension. He turned the phrase "stirs a
chivalrous passion" over and over in his mind. It united again
and again with the luminous image of the girl until a pattern
of symbols completing a poem flowed over him like musical
configurations of fading coals:

> The radiant memory of your
> brown, smoldering eyes
> stirs a chivalrous passion,
> oh, my much praised,
> bashful, loveless and sexless
> gentle donna,
> like an August breeze
> lingering above olive trees,
> the breath of an evening almost gone.

He spoke the lines aloud several times before pausing to write them down. He stayed at the window repeating the lines to himself, enchanted by the feeling of warmth they gave him. It was not until birds began chattering and the sky brightened that he finally went to bed.

He slept a few hours, then got up for his ten o'clock class. If not for this being the last class before midterms, he probably would have just gone ahead and slept in. Vaguely conscious he was running late, he left the house without thinking to see if the girl across the street might be leaving, too. It was not until he heard a car horn blaring at him that he realized he was crossing an intersection and he suddenly caught a glimpse of her reddish hair just ahead of him in the intersection. She whirled around at the car, then saw David staring at her. The horn honked again, and David jumped out of the way, almost bumping into the girl.

"Are you all right?" she asked.

"One step from the twilight zone, I guess," David responded, not quite sure he was not already there. He glanced at her eyes and saw they were hazel, then her lips and saw that they were more red than he had imagined. He realized he had never been this close to her and suddenly felt silly about the fantasy he had been focusing upon his inaccurate image of what she looked like.

"I've been there—nice place to visit, but I wouldn't want to take up permanent residence." She smiled and resumed crossing the intersection. David began walking behind her, looking at her feet, admiring the crisp, confident way she marked the pavement, then noticing a clean, iris-like scent that trailed her figure like an invisible wake. "Were you following me again?" she asked over her shoulder without looking at him.

He tried not to break stride, but it didn't work. He tripped over the curb. He did not know what to say.

She turned around frowning and said, "Well, were you?"

"Uhh, no," David said, glancing first at her eyes, then over her shoulder. "I was just sleepwalking to class, I think."

"But you've followed me before, haven't you?"

David took a deep breath and let it out slowly, then said, "Yes."

"Hmph. Well, at least you're honest. A little shy, maybe, and perhaps too obsessive for your own good, but that's nothing new. You like classical music, don't you?"

"Yes," David answered. As they began walking toward the school buildings, she explained that Friday night some musician friends of hers would be playing at The Alcove, a small open-air theater in a nearby park, and she wanted someone to go with. She said she needed someone to walk her home afterwards. Before he really grasped what was happening, his mouth started talking again.

"Oh, yeah! I mean, Christ yeah! I mean I'd be happy to . . . real happy. But, uh . . . I . . . I have an exam that night. That's tomorrow night, isn't it?"

She nodded.

"Yeah, well, like I said, I've got an exam, so I . . . can't. But I could rush through it and meet you there."

All of his sparkling, pre-planned conversations were hopelessly tangled in a garbled knot. While he spoke she looked straight into his eyes and smiled. A group of students passed by talking amongst themselves. Then the two of them were alone on a path between two buildings. She leaned against a railing, running her fingers through the designs of flowers and vines imprinted on it. A beam of sunlight caught the pale curve of her shoulder and fell across her arm, following the curve of her waist, and lit up her hand upon the railing. She stood and paused, as if listening to a voice in her mind, or perhaps the silence, then said, "Good. Then I'll see you Friday night."

"I . . . I don't know your name."

"You ought to. It's Elizabeth. I know yours—David. You can call me Liz. Try not to be too late, all right?"

He nodded and muttered "Yes" as she passed through a gate and out of sight.

A torrent of thoughts and emotions swept over David, laying waste his waking and sleeping moments after that meeting. He relived each second of their encounter, prying every possible meaning from everything she said, each gesture, each nuance, her mood, the light in her eyes. He wished he could eliminate the tedious intervening minutes and hours. He could not study without becoming absorbed into the musical quality of her voice or the anticipation of what he could say when he met her again. The next day the classes seemed interminable. His instructors made dull meaningless sounds, and his books seemed like dreary masses of monotonous symbols. He had hardly any patience with the midterm papers that were due. All the problems of school seemed unreal and divorced from what was truly vital and fascinating.

Friday afternoon he went to his European History instructor and asked him how long he expected the exam to take. He was grading term papers with a sour frown on his face, and without looking up, answered: "I don't know. More than two hours, less than four hours. There's several essays at the end that may take some time. That's all I can tell you." He acted as if he had been answering the same question all day. David left the building in a foul mood and walked slowly toward his apartment.

At seven o'clock, he heard the voices of students leaving and the door slamming. He knew it was time to go. He picked up his notebook and pens and walked quickly to the door. He gave his room one final approving glance, in case he got lucky, and shut the door, then left the house.

The fresh evening air invigorated him and he began to feel adventurous and high-spirited. He gripped his notebook tightly and strode down Green Street toward the history building. The sight of sidewalks filled with nervous students evoked a sensation of belonging to a centuries-old ritual of midterm testing of which this evening was but one link of the entire concatenation. He felt as if he were following some preordained pattern, a perennially repeated pattern in which each student's predicament was actually following and contributing to this kaleidoscopic design. As he entered the building, this transporting sense of déjà vu soothed him and reinforced his fascination with Elizabeth, as he felt he was pursuing something akin to fate.

He went straight to the exam room and took a seat in the front row. After an unbearable delay, the instructor appeared with copies of the exams in his arms. He placed them on a table and whispered something to one of his teaching assistants. David glanced at the clock and wished they would hurry. The instructor climbed up on the stage and waited for the noises of papers rustling, students whispering and doors shutting to die down. David looked at the clock three times before the instructor began giving the directions for the exams.

"All right. Listen up. There will be three parts to this exam. The first two parts are timed tests, taking 45 minutes each. The third consists of three essays which you may spend as much time with as you like."

David began computing how long the exam would take, figuring it would take a little over two hours. He smiled, deciding to be out by 9:45.

"The teaching assistants will pass out the exams, but when you get them, do not start until I say to."

Three teaching assistants walked over to the exam forms and picked them up. They were in no hurry and walked up the aisles slowly handing out the forms. David took his, wrote his name on it, and hunched over ready to start.

The first two exams seemed to pass quickly. He was shocked when he saw that the clock said 9:15. He became nervous, anxious to get the exam over with. His hands trembled and his high-spirited confidence began to waver as a desperate sinking sensation grew in his chest. By the time the essay questions were passed out, his mind was clouded. The image of Elizabeth growing tired of waiting, then walking home alone, raised mixtures of anguish, anger and apathy. He sat staring at the first question well over five minutes before he forced himself to start writing. It was 9:40 when he finished the essay. He started the next question immediately, but glanced at the clock every five minutes while he wrote it. It was quarter past ten when he handed in his exam. He walked quickly out of the room, fearing she had already left.

The park was nearly three blocks from the history building. When he passed out the door, he quickened his pace, still hoping she would be there waiting. The street was nearly empty. At the corner of the second block, a boy and a girl stood whispering to each other, leaning their shoulders together and laughing. He heard bits of their conversation as he passed them. The girl pushed the boy's hand off her hip.

"Aren't you the tease!" the boy said.

"You started it."

"Who did? You're the one who tripped me and tried to beat me to the ground."

"That's not true." She grabbed his head and kissed him on the lips and they laughed.

David ran across the street pretending not to notice them. He could hear the indistinct sounds of music and laughter echoing from the bars on Green Street. When he reached the park, the sidewalks were completely empty. There was no evening breeze brushing the trees. He recognized the silence as that which pervades a school room after every one has gone home. As he approached The Alcove, he could see a few people gathered on the benches that lined the path. There was no music.

In a far corner, leaning against the arm of a stone bench, was a girl gazing at something in her hands. Her dimly lit silhouette would have been unrecognizable to anyone but David. A warm rush flowed over him. He did not speak. Her head was bent and she looked as if she were praying. The moon glowed on her skin, revealing a nymph-like quality in her figure. Her hair was tied loosely behind her neck. It was several seconds before she lifted her head and saw David staring at her.

David expected her to say something, but when she did not, he said, "Sorry I'm late. The exam took a bit longer than I thought it would."

"I knew you'd say that. That's fine. I wish you could have been here for the music—it was really beautiful. You know Tom? He's such an ass, but he plays the recorder so perfectly. I can't believe it, you know what I mean?"

"Hm-hmm. You mean Tom Caines?"

"Yeah."

"How do you know him?"

"He went to high school with my brother, Chris."

"Oh."

The stilted silence swelled between them as David thought of, then eliminated, things to say. Elizabeth motioned to the bench and said, "Here, sit down. How'd your exam go?"

"Fine. It was a piece of cake—it just took too long."

"That's okay. Don't worry about it."

David sat, one leg bent and propping up his chin, thinking how to express what she inspired. She wore a pale blue dress that was tight from her shoulders down to her waist, then pleated over her hips, finally resting in a series of loose folds about her knees. Her eyes seemed illuminated by a gently shaded lamp hidden deep within her. She lifted her knee up to her chest and leaned her cheek on it, mimicking David. She looked at David's hands clasped beneath his chin.

"How did you know my name?" he asked.

"I asked Tom. He said your name was David Kitt. I'd seen you leaving your house and suspected you actually followed me each morning. I became curious and decided to find out about you. I pointed you out to Tom and he said you ate at the same dining hall. He said you were moody and that you were here on some sort of writing scholarship. I thought I recognized you, but I wasn't sure. I started watching you and then I got it."

"Got what?"

"Well . . . I remembered, but you don't have to believe me if you don' t want to. It was a long time ago. Your name was Chris . . . Chris Marlowe. Mine was Elizabeth. You called me Liz. I called you Kit. You wrote poetry and plays. I was a barmaid and you wanted me to quit and run away to the country with you, but I wouldn't. We were poor. You were very lovely—outspoken and romantic. A man named Frazer said I was an expensive, godless whore, and no wonder you couldn't pay the rent. You threw your beer mug at him and began shouting. He pulled out a dagger and chased you around the tables. You'd nearly wrecked the place before you tripped. He lunged and stabbed you in the head. That was 1593. You were 29. I was heartbroken."

David could not speak. Chills ran up and down his spine, and tears began to smear his vision. He could not tell whether the light in her eyes was the warm glow of affinity or the spark of insanity.

"I know it's sort of hard to believe, sounds crazy and so forth, but I see these things, you know, and well . . . you still write poetry, don't you?"

He nodded. "The radiant memory of your brown smoldering eyes stirs a chivalrous passion, oh, my much praised, bashful, loveless and sexless gentle donna, like an August breeze lingering above olive trees, the breath of an evening almost gone."

Elizabeth listened intently while David muttered the poem. As it penetrated her effervescent sociability, she bent her head near David's and kissed him on the lips. Her lips were warm and moist. She started to lift her head, but sighed, and kissed him again, longer and harder. Then she sat back and closed her eyes.

"That was nice. So delicate."

After several moments, she stood up, pulling David behind her. "Come on. Let's go."

She pulled his hand around her waist and guided him to the path leading out of the park. They walked by lovers whispering to each other in the shadows of low tree limbs beneath a streetlamp. There were rows of houses, then storefronts. They walked past art galleries and laundromats, saying almost nothing, not really needing to speak. Behind them was a group of noisy drunks singing, "Let's get drunk and go naked, let's get drunk and go na-ked." The two of them smiled to each other and laughed. When they arrived at her gate, he said, "Tomorrow night?"

"Uh," Elizabeth paused and looked at David, then smiled, she nodded her head and said, "Yeah sure, tomorrow night."

He kissed her again and ran across the street and into his apartment. He left the room dark, preferring to feel his way to his stereo. He switched it on and placed a set of recordings of Rachmani-noff's preludes and concertos on the spindle. Then he relaxed on his bed, lying awake, thinking about Elizabeth and what she had said. After two discs had played, he sat up and turned on the lamp. He pulled a piece of paper off his desk, and began writing:

And tonight
she walked beside me
past the art galleries
and laundromats.
Once her hand
brushed mine.
I watched her hair
blown by
the crisp autumn wind.
She said she lived alone
and I let it pass
unnoticed.

He did not read it over, but leaned back into his pillow and fell asleep with his clothes on.

The next morning he woke up, anxious to see Elizabeth again. He spent a few hours in the library reading about Christopher Marlowe. After lunch, he decided to take a walk. He walked along his usual path, his thoughts wandering between the possibilities and facets of past lives and the details of houses or trees or statues he had somehow never noticed before. He finally arrived at a pond circled with benches and tables for playing chess. He was not hungry and he spent a good part of the afternoon lying in the sun trying to imagine more of his past. As the sun reached into the trees, David wrote another poem:

Sunday morning's
loves
lie
listlessly
around the park,
while slowly through
the leaves and branches
on the bald streets
breaks the blushed dawn.

He folded the paper he had been scribbling on and put it in his shirt pocket, then began walking home.

When he got back to campus, it was nearly dusk. The air was becoming brisk and some of the streetlights had already come on. David went straight to the cafeteria. He got the last serving of fish and the last dessert. He sat down in a quiet corner at a table by himself. He picked at the dinner. He could hear several students arguing amongst themselves. He listened vaguely, occasionally catching bits of their contentions. As he was about to leave, Tom shouted out his name.

"Kitt! Hey, Kitt!" He called out to David with a snide grin on his face. "Hey . . . I saw you with Liz Graham last night. She's crazy, you know. A cross between a religious fanatic and a nymphomaniac. I scored with her a few times, but she called it off because I didn't believe in past lives. She goes around telling people who they were—you know, Napoleon, Beethoven. She said I was a sort of court musician who screwed Mary, Queen of Scots. Bunch of shit, if you ask me. She's nuts."

David sat motionless. His thoughts raced past the memories of her figure before him each morning, to the light in her eyes in the park, to her face contorted and gasping beneath Caines' body, then hard and indignant as she told him to get out. Caines' voice had pierced him like a cold sword. He stood up, his hands trembling and his eyes stinging. He shivered and burned with humiliation. The image of the spark in Elizabeth's eyes became all too clear. In the silence, David's heart withered like a poisoned flower. He saw Caines' grin through a confusion of anger and a swelling grief. Before he was conscious of moving, a rush of tables, faces and arms, frenzied voices, the sensation of his fist smashing into Caines' face, Caines' body collapsing unconscious on the floor, converged in a single delirious event. He threw off the frantic grip of Caines' friends, then fled the cafeteria, alone.

He ran to his apartment in a violent grief. He turned on his stereo and collapsed on his bed. He made a futile attempt to be devoted, but the feeling of betrayal and ridicule consumed it like tinder in a raging flame. He passed between consciousness and unconsciousness for nearly an hour. Eventually consciousness began ebbing back over him slowly, from what seemed like a vast distance. His head was immersed in a dull, sourceless ache. He became aware of the scene around him: the dusty odors, Rachmaninoff's Second Piano Concerto, the books strewn about, the scraps of paper and poems on his desk. David sat up and opened a drawer in his desk. He rummaged around until he found and pulled out a candle. He lit it and stared at the flame for a few minutes, then he picked up the poems, and without looking at them, put them into the flame. He watched the curls of smoke weave in and out of the candlelight, dancing up to the ceiling. Then he smiled, having decided to drink himself to sleep.

Elizabeth

ELIZABETH lived by herself, or more accurately, with herself, in a moderately attractive, furnished one-bedroom apartment: moderate due to her student status, attractive due to her compulsive desire to make an arts and crafts gallery out of wherever she lived. The walls of every room of the apartment, save those of the shower stall, were covered with collages, theater bills, paintings, drawings, film posters, hanging plants, old parlor mirrors (three of those, plus a full-length mirror on the door to her closet), and assorted photographs culled from magazines and newspapers, alongside meticulously detailed batiks and welded metal sculptures.

There were little platitudes posted here and there. One, "Cleanliness is next to godliness," was beneath a picture of Fred Astaire dancing with Ginger Rogers in one of her white lamé gowns. In Elizabeth's mind, there was something clean and perfect and sacred about their dancing. "Clean" connoted a freedom from impurities, from self-indulgence, unstained in a metaphysical sense, rather than simply "recently laundered." She knew that the word, at its heart, meant bright and pure. From this it was a small step, in her kind of logic, to turn the stale aphorism into a kind of mantra, somehow attached to the image of Astaire and Rogers' dancing.

There were other sayings around the room or taped to her mirrors. One was beneath a picture of an impoverished Virginia Cherrill collapsed with grief at having dropped a bottle of milk, while Charlie Chaplin was perched on the gutter trying to crawl in her second story window with a roll of cash bulging in his back pocket. Printed like a film subtitle was "Never cry over spilled milk." Some were merely quotes from books she had liked. Others were warnings to mend some fault she was trying to correct in herself. All in all, they seemed like notes left by forbearing angels to an incurably absent-minded saint.

It was from this world that Elizabeth emerged daily, still emanating an aura of eccentricity. Today, however, she had not emerged as yet, in spite of the fact that it was clearly a beautiful day waning toward its sunset. She had spent the day painting in her room, fantasizing about her evening out with David. Several times, after a spell of daydreaming, she sang aloud without any conscious purpose, "Somewhere the sun is shining, so honey don't you cry, look for the silver lining, the clouds will soon roll by." She was happy and more than content to just sit in her room musing all day, which is more or less what she did until around dinnertime, when she went to her refrigerator and found it virtually empty.

"Oh Christ," she said, "now I have to go to that damn meat market by myself. During mating season. Male to female ratio at rush hour—five to one. Not a pretty picture." She swung the refrigerator door shut. "On the other hand, I could probably trick Sam into going with me. And besides, I think I'm beginning to show signs of cabin fever—isolation dementia—" She turned around to the telephone and began dialing, still mid-conversation with herself. "Kill two birds with one stone, old girl, safety and companionship. By God, you are clever sometimes. Not very often, but you have your moments, kiddo—Hello, Sam?"

The deeper, matronizing voice of a woman somewhere beyond thirty-five answered, "Sorry dear, no Sams here—must be a wrong connection."

"Oh, come on, Sam—"

"Melinda's the name. To whom on earth do you think you're speaking?"

"Sam—"

"Melinda. And if you don't mind your p's and q's, it'll be Mrs. Spade to you."

"Sammie—how can I call you a decent, loving nickname with a lemon for a starter like Melinda?"

"I think it's a lovely name."

"Goddamn it! So do I. So do I. I love your name, but I can't stand the formality of always calling you Melinda, and Mellie is too bovine. My god, if—"

"All right, already. I see the light. What can I do for you this evening?"

"My refrigerator's empty—"

"Now that is a problem."

"Oh, come on, Sam. Be a good girl and go shopping with me. I can't bear the thought of going into that toad den by myself. It's practically dusk, you know, and I haven't a thing to eat."

"All right, you talked me into it. I need a little more hair of the cur dog anyway. Meet ya at the corner."

"OK, see ya."

Five minutes later they met at the corner about a block from Elizabeth's apartment. It was getting darker out, or one might think of it as losing light. Sam appeared shortly after Elizabeth got there. She was taller and older than Elizabeth. She looked like a pretty girl who had gained weight, not too much, but past the point of being slender. She wore a calf-length cotton dress and a very loose brassiere. She strolled with an amiable lack of self-consciousness that carried through to the comfortable swirling motion that the hem of her dress made about her legs. They greeted each other warmly, and for the four or five blocks to the store, Sam dished the latest on her former husband and sometime lover, Jack.

Contrary to Elizabeth's concerns, their journey through the store passed uneventfully. Elizabeth picked out the usual staples plus several frozen dinners, some fruit and salad mixings, but nobody tried to help her buy cucumbers or bananas. Sam bought a six pack of beer. As they walked out of the store, Sam opened one of the cans and said, after noting the uneventfulness of their trip, "Elizabeth, darling, it's high time you either get a little braver or you get married."

"Married?" Elizabeth snorted. "I haven't even finished college yet. I can't be going off getting married—it isn't natural."

Sam laughed. "Sure you can. You're just procrastinating. I've been married and divorced and practically married again in the time you've spent deciding whether to amass another year's credits or just go ahead and graduate."

"But you're different."

"Well what about this Caines? Tom. He looked all right to me."

"Tom is an ass. I couldn't marry him—it'd be sodomy. And besides . . ." Elizabeth blushed.

"And besides what, honey? Don't let the cat hold your tongue—you're in safe company."

"And besides, I think I'm in love."

At this, Sam spewed a mouthful of beer and started laughing out loud. She put her hand on Elizabeth's shoulder to keep her from crossing the parking lot and to support herself while she laughed.

"What's so damn funny? I'm not kidding—it's true."

"I think," Sam gasped between sobs, "I don't know—I think it's that note of sincerity against the image of the last six or seven boyfriends you've run through."

"I haven't had any boyfriends, darling. Just persons of the opposite sex with whom I've had social engagements. Dates. Mighty insipid ones at that. Sometimes you infuriate me, Sam. Any half-witted imbecile could clearly see that—"

"They were superficial sexual encounters, mere training exercises for the big one, bla bla bla. Why, just last week, you were playing peeping Tom with that kid across the street." Elizabeth smiled sheepishly and shrugged. Sam gently brushed some wisps of hair from Elizabeth's eyes. "Oh, I see. I see. I'm beginning to get the smoke signals now. It's that kid across the street . . . the one you thought had an awful crush on you, isn't it? So you decided to 'encounter' him, eh?"

Elizabeth nodded and said, "Hm-hm." Whatever hostility had bristled the air around her a moment earlier was now gone. They began crossing the parking lot again, strolling down the middle of the driveway, not really paying attention to any traffic that might be approaching. "It's just lovely. Love at first sight, I swear. He's so perfect. He writes simply beautiful poetry. I know what he's thinking, what he's feeling. It's like an extrasensory perception. Like . . . like. Well, I don't know. His eyes. He's—"

Just at that moment, Sam turned her head to watch a tall, good-looking man, dressed down in blue jeans and a worn leather jacket, cross in front of them and open the door to a blood-red Jaguar sedan.

"Well get a load of this one, honey."

Elizabeth looked and was conspicuously enchanted, so much so that she failed to notice that she was stepping into an oil spill. About the point where her right foot reached her left shoulder, the groceries flew out of her arm and scattered. Her impact with the asphalt was cushioned by a loaf of wheat bread and a carton of eggs, so she was not hurt very much. Two cans of tuna fish and a jar of mayonnaise continued rolling down the sidewalk and for several seconds the aura of turmoil hung about her.

Elizabeth muttered, "Goddamn it! Now that's just not fair. Nice bodies were made to be looked at."

Sam bent over to give her a hand and said, "What's that?"

"Just me and myself having a bit of a tiff, dear," she said as she gathered herself up off the ground. "Don't worry that good Samaritan soul of yours about me. I'm quite all right. I wasn't looking at him, really. It was his goddamn car. What a disgusting color to paint such a wonderful car." She smoothed out her dress and began picking the eggshells off of it.

"Sometimes, Liz old girl," Sam said while helping Elizabeth pick some pieces off the back of her pants, "I have to admit, you're far and away my favorite actress."

Elizabeth smiled and curtsied and said, "Why, thank you," affecting her brand of modesty. Sam laughed and they both began gathering up the scattered groceries.

When Sam brought the last stray can of tuna fish, she remarked, "You don't hold anything back when you fall for 'em, you just dive right in, don't ya, honey?"

"Ho, ho." Elizabeth sneered and pretended to ignore Sam as she looked around making sure they'd found everything, then said, "OK, let's get goin'. I've got a social engagement this evening."

Sam smiled and started off. The two of them walked slowly towards their apartments through a tunnel of dark trees. The street lights were just coming on and the streets were empty and quiet. Neither of the two friends spoke for the first two blocks from the parking lot. They were close enough to have acquired the convention of mutual silence at times. Not that they were moody or resentful, but that they did not have to be continually entertaining to each other. Elizabeth seemed to be daydreaming. Sam was enchanted by the gold leaves above their heads and about their feet. They were very comfortable together.

As they crossed the street after the third block, Elizabeth said, as if there had been no silence, "There's a difference between love and fascination, you know."

Sam replied, almost *non sequitur*, "Do you think it might be serious with this—"

"David."

"—get serious with this David, or what?"

"Sam, I may be flaky, but I'm not stupid," she said, pretending not to have already considered it. "You know how they're always coming up with some intolerable quirk or some disgusting bias. And then I don't care anymore. It takes a while for the real man to shine through the performance. How was I to know Tom was an ass till the next morning. And Christ, I haven't made love to David yet—I've only kissed him once or twice—"

"That's a record."

"Now God damn it, that's just not fair—"

"OK. OK. I'm not saying you shouldn't make love. On the contrary, I think you *should* make love. Keeping that sort of energy packed away isn't good for you. I think it releases bad chemicals into your bloodstream. Makes you act strange."

"Don't you like the way I act?"

"I think your acting's fine, dear—it's you I'm worried about. Besides, sex appears to be one of the few areas of your life free from pro-" Elizabeth tried to elbow Sam in the ribs, but Sam gracefully, and without missing a step, dodged her, "-crastination."

"Thanks a lot, pal."

"Take it as a compliment."

"Oh, yeah. Right. Thanks"

"You're welcome." Sam leaned towards Elizabeth, and they bumped shoulders affectionately. "Well, here's my corner. You have a nice night out, honey, and save me some of the luscious details, all right?"

"OK. G'night, Sam."

"G'night, Liz."

When Elizabeth got back to her apartment, she immediately began making dinner with what groceries had survived. She made a tuna melt and ate it without sitting down, leaving the dishes in the sink. It was nearly 7:00 by then, so she had to start getting dressed to be ready by eight. And, though she did not have much time, she simply had to take a shower, cleanliness being next to godliness, and that night she intended to look divine.

She'd showered quickly despite having washed her hair and shaved her legs. She stepped out of the stall singing "Night and Day" and dried off with a black towel. After wrapping the towel around her head, she threw on a turquoise kimono with gold embroidered dragons on it. Still humming the song to herself, she sat in front of a small vanity cluttered with hair and make-up brushes, antique perfume bottles, vials of aromatic oils, cosmetic cream jars, and trays of eye shadow. About twenty nail polish bottles were lined up like a color chart in the middle, making the mirror look like an easel surrounded by a loosely organized, slightly disheveled painter's palette with specks of eye shadow, powder and cream splattered about it. A picture of her mother taped to the mirror caught Elizabeth's eye and she spoke to it aloud as she began applying moisturizer to her face.

"Mother, dear Mother. Lord knows I've tried to be good, but I'm incorrigible, a hopeless case. A lost cause from the moment I fell down those awful basement stairs and landed right on my ever-loving feline feet. I should have been hurt—not wounded, madam, but dead. So from that point on, I've known my life's been charmed, and there's no sense trying to convince me otherwise."

She leaned toward the mirror and without a downward glance, picked up an eyeliner and deftly painted black lines along her upper and lower eyelids with four swift strokes. She brushed a small amount of mascara on her eyelashes and dabbed a nearly invisible layer of blue-green eye shadow on her upper eyelids, enough to accent without being conspicuous. She had already painted her relatively short nails about the same color the day before, so they only needed minor touch-up. Her hair was still wet under the towel, so she unhooked a blow-dryer hanging from the side of the vanity, simultaneously flipped the towel off and the blow-dryer on, and ran a brush through her thick reddish hair until it made clean, dry lines sweeping away from her face. After that, she slipped two glazed dark blue combs into her hair above her ears, held her nails up to her face and leaned into the mirror to see how the various shades of blue and aqua matched.

Satisfied with the match, she walked over to her dresser and picked out some black seamed pantyhose and a black bra. She sat down at the vanity again, rolled the nylons down then pulled them up, one leg at a time, careful to keep the seams running down the center of her calves. She shrugged off the kimono and slipped the bra over her small, slightly rounded breasts, around which she smeared drops of an earthy-smelling rose oil. She dabbed the vial of oil against her lower neck and chest, then rubbed the droplets in with her wrist and palm.

Looking, and perhaps feeling, a little like a dark-haired version of Marlene Dietrich's "Blue Angel," she glided over to the closet and pulled out a shimmery indigo-colored dress that appeared silken, but was actually rayon, which she referred to as her "dancing dress." She had made it herself, fashioned after one of the real silk dresses Irene Castle used to wear when she toured Europe and turned early twentieth-century fashion and formal dancing upside down. Its fluid, somewhat lingerie-like quality had been risqué then, but was merely suggestive now. She slipped it on and stepped in front of her full-length mirror, looking at her profile from head to toe. Frowning disparagingly, she said, "Look at that girl, will ya? Practically flat-chested." She turned around to face the mirror and tapped herself on the chin. "Yah, but get that gleam in her eye, that's what knocks 'em dead. A real comely wench, you might even say she's—mmm—provocative."

She changed her voice to remark, "You might, but I'd just say she's pixilated."

Elizabeth as Elizabeth looked down her nose at her imaginary critic and snorted, "Humph!" then stalked out of the mirror.

At 8:30, Elizabeth sat in her living room looking out the window waiting for David. He was supposed to have been there at eight. He only lived across the street, so Lord knew what was taking him. She ordinarily would have started some small project like writing a letter or sketching people that walked by—and might even have forgotten about the date altogether. She had listened to both sides of Artie Shaw's Big Band recordings. She had already fooled around with an unfinished portrait, balancing some light greens in the background with light green highlights in the folds of a dress in the middle ground, careful to keep the paint off of her own dress. Having finished that, there was nothing left to do. It was time to go. The music had stopped playing, she was dressed up, she was pretty, and she was ready to leave, so she grabbed a sweater and left her apartment to go get him.

Fall had a peculiarly invigorating effect on Elizabeth. The blends of reds, yellows, and oranges seemed to match her concept of how the universe should look, particularly in light of the new love affair she was caught up in. David's house was a large Victorian built around the turn of the century. It wasn't really David's house—he just had a room there—but it was David's house as far as she was concerned. As she came up the walk, she could see only one light on in the first floor where he stayed. No one answered the front door. Undaunted, she went around back to tap on his window. The walk to the back was a good deal darker than out front, and she grew a little scared.

She began tiptoeing as she came up to his bedroom window.

It was beginning to get chilly and her hands were becoming noticeably cold. The dim reflection of light from a tree seemed unnatural and other-worldly. She tapped on the window once but got no answer. She tapped again, watching the clouds of smoke rush out of her mouth. She made a circle out of her lips and tried to blow smoke rings. Still no answer. Throwing all protocol aside, she gave the window a couple of good bangs.

Finally, someone came to the window. She could barely see the face in the dark, but recognized it as David's when he turned a small reading light on. She could see he looked grim. His hair was messed, his eyes seemed to have dark rings under them, his shirt was unbuttoned, and he was unshaven. She motioned for him to open the window, which he did after turning the light off again.

"Hey—we've got a date!"

David did not say anything. She knew he was a little too serious, so was not surprised by his silence.

"You know—me and you—us—we have a date, remember?"

David slowly rubbed his hand along the side of his face, feeling the pull of his whiskers. He looked over her shoulder into some imaginary distance. He seemed to squint. He took a short breath, which he let out slowly, then said, "I called it off."

"Called it off? Called it off! You can't do that. Dates with me are immutable acts of God, willed by Krishna, planned and recorded in the Akashic Records, executed by hosts of exalted angels—no, you can't break a date with me. As far as they're concerned, it has already happened."

"Oh, I see. Do I bow or genuflect, your highness?"

"Just say three Hail Mary's and beg forgiveness," she retorted without thinking, affecting a sweet piety. But the thrill of the cleverness wore thin quickly, and she paused to examine him more closely. "David, what's the matter with you?"

"Nothing."

"David, I'm not joking now—what's wrong? You're very bitter about something. What is it?"

"There's nothing wrong, really. Except—except I think it's better if we, you and I, don't take this any further."

"Come on—what's wrong?"

"Nothing!"

"Come on, tell me."

"Really, there's nothing to tell."

"OK. I'm coming in there and staying in until you tell me!"

She grabbed the window sill and started climbing in through the window. David moved back, shaking his head, having obtained objective, immutable proof that she really was, as he previously suspected, not playing with a full set of marbles.

Once in, Elizabeth looked around the dim candlelit room. There were a few books lying on the floor, some clothes piled on a chair in the corner, a liberal assortment of magazine and newspaper photographs on the wall above his bed, and a large desk covered with innumerable folders, piles of papers, a fountain pen and a couple of bottles of ink, two unidentifiable plants, a desk calendar, and three candles, one of them lit. The room smelled like a mixture of incense, tobacco, and old books. From the dark space of the darkest corner came music from an almost invisible stereo. Elizabeth sat down in a chair facing the back of the room. She crossed her legs and stared out the window.

After several minutes she said, "Rachmaninoff?"

"Hm-hmm."

"Second piano concerto, last movement."

"Hm-hmm." David sat down on his bed, sitting across from Elizabeth. His right hand was fumbling with a pack of cigarettes while she sat, silent. He put a cigarette in the side of his mouth and lit it. He blew a stream of smoke toward the candle, then leaned back disinterestedly on his pillow. Elizabeth turned to look at him. He purposely avoided looking at her. Several more minutes passed before she ventured to say anything more.

"Are you going to tell me, or what?"

"There's nothing to tell." He tapped his cigarette over his free hand.

Exasperated, she turned back to face the window.

"You're lying."

"I'm not lying. Really. It would be better if you just left right now."

There was a note of finality in his voice that Elizabeth chose to ignore. "I know you're lying, and I'm not leaving until you tell me what's going on." She uncrossed her legs and sat upright. "Who've you been talking to?"

David pulled an ashtray off the desk and flicked a dangerously long ash into it. "I'm not saying anything about anyone."

"Oh, so you did talk to someone. What'd he, she or it say? It must have been pretty bad—eating babies or voting Republican or something, you know."

David laughed and glanced at her. "I've just decided not to continue our relationship. That's all."

"That's all! That's all?" She looked up and addressed the ceiling, "Is this another one of your goddamn tricks?"

David turned over and stared at her. "What are you doing? Who are you talking to?"

Elizabeth continued facing the ceiling, then she looked down a few seconds, considering how to say what she now had to say.

"My guardian angel, " she deadpanned. "We have a very intimate relationship. I tell him jokes and make fun of him, and he makes jokes out of my life. It's a positively divine game. Every once in a while I let him know I'm onto one of his plans, just to poke a hole in his balloon, if you know what I mean—keep him from getting too hoity-toity about this big trick he thinks he's going to surprise me with—you don't believe me, do you? Well, neither do I half the time, so what difference does it make?"

David was looking at her, but not saying anything. He took a couple of long drags from his cigarette before tapping the growing ash. He tried to make out the expression on her face, but could not. He could just see the glow in her eyes. "Caines told me you're a cross between a religious fanatic and a nymphomaniac."

"And before that, I was an expensive, godless whore, so what does he know? And you believed him, right? Nothing like a little loyalty." She faced the window a few moments then abruptly faced David. "You know, that guy is the type that keeps a graph of the number of women he seduces per month under his pillow, right next to his 8x10 black and white glossy of himself."

Elizabeth turned back to the window and exhaled long and slowly as she sank lower into her chair. "Well, that's my Tommie," she mused, "no bitterness, no recrimination—just a good swift left to the jaw. I used to be 'a sensual girl with just the right touch of mystical sensitivity.' He told me that. But then, of course, that sort of thing was fashionable. The mystical sensitivity. I believed him. So what? You got another cigarette?"

David pulled a cigarette out of his pack and groped around for the book of matches. When she turned around to get them, he noticed the glint of candlelight in the glazed comb in her hair. He could not see her eyes. She took the cigarette and lit it without looking at him. The smoke drifted above her head; caught in the candlelight, it looked like an ethereal emanation from her body. For a moment, her silhouette seemed to sway in and out of the light, as if she were dancing.

"He said you go around telling everyone they're Beethoven or Napoleon or something, you know."

"That's a bit of an exaggeration. I've never met either of them. So that's just not true."

"What about this Christopher Marlowe business?"

"Well that's different. I can't help it if it seems true. It's just something I can perceive, sort of. I think people are kind of caught in a web of experiences with each other which they relive together until they resolve them. Over and over. Like a fugue or a kaleidoscope—wearing bodies like masks, acting out variations of the same drama. Sometimes I can see past the masks. I could lie about it or pretend not to notice. Would that be better?"

"Yeah." David stared at his hands clasped in front of his knees. "No. I don't know. I don't know. You have to admit that you're pretty goddamned weird, and I guess some would call it crazy—whimsical at best. Goddamned unusual, in any case."

Elizabeth did not respond. David reached for the pack of Marlboros and pulled out another cigarette. He lit it with a match and the phosphorescent glow lit up his face for a second.

"I fully intended to stand you up tonight—you know, give you the old deep-six, the one-two, sayonara, see you around sweetheart." He was not looking at her. He was looking at the tip of his third cigarette, his attention focused on the smoldering reds and oranges burning radiantly in the dark. "I don't think he's right. Caines, that is. He's—I've never liked him. He gives me headaches and makes me mad."

Elizabeth said nothing. He could not tell whether she had merely accepted what he said, or was silently angry. She took a couple of long drags from her cigarette and appeared to be listening to the stereo. When the last record ended, she got up to play them again. There was very little light, but her eyes were accustomed to it by then. She came back to her chair slowly and sat down. She rested her chin on her palm pensively, looking vaguely in David's direction.

He was lying on the bed, looking at the ceiling. She could see the profile of his face—his left hand behind his head, the pack of cigarettes beside him. Her cigarette was near the filter, so she reached over to the dish holding the candle and put it out. Around the candle were ashes of burned paper, like fragile sculptures of ancient scrolls. She picked one up, careful to keep it from collapsing between her fingers. She held it close to her face a few moments, then set it down. The light from the candle made her skin gold. She looked back at David more intently, as if studying the lines and angles of his skeletal structure, with the different curves and figures giving a rhythm to the static image of his body. Her face showed no expression.

"You burned that poem."

David said nothing. An emanation of smoke hung over his hand, twirling up from the cigarette's red tip. "More than one."

"That was pretty stupid." The bitterness with which she said "stupid" pierced David, and the open-hearted feeling he had begun to feel again started to fold and wither like a flower that feels a storm approaching from a distance.

"I thought maybe you were—you were like Caines said."

"Like I—"

"Like you were doing it on purpose, teasing—that you really were—"

"A religious fanatic and a nymphomaniac. A horny flake."

"Hm-hmm." David was facing her, half-in and half-out of the candlelight. She waited for "Variations on a Theme by Paganini" to finish before she spoke again.

"Well, it's true, in a way. But not the way he thinks. Some people don't want to submit to the demands of enlightened religion, but don't want to abandon it altogether, either. I love beauty, passion, movies, pretty clothes—but I'm not altogether committed to them. In between. Renounced and criticized by both the mundane and the enlightened, or at least dedicated. My brother thinks I'm a religious hypocrite—a self-indulgent dilettante. So what do I do? Quit falling in love? Forget Fred and Ginger? Never get drunk again? Go celibate? If I were going to get really ascetic and pure about it, that's what I'd have to do—sacrifice all the mundane pleasures for the beatific bliss that's always there that we're only distracted from by our incontinent senses. I know enough about that sort of stuff, the Four Noble Truths and all, to be out on the street proselytizing with the best of them. But I don't. I like being pretty. I like being smart. I like being admired. I like admiring beauty. So here I am. And here you are, too, or at least I thought so." She stopped and looked at David, checking to see if he'd been listening to her. Then she turned away and said nothing for perhaps a minute, not expecting him to reply, as though weighing a number of never-spoken thoughts before disclosing them to a possibly critical audience. She was unaware of the darkness and the cold and the silence in the room. She sighed and leaned into the back of her chair.

"Sometimes certain people, or things, are the keys that unlock the place where you love. Where you *are* love. It's sort of magical and delicate. When two people do it for each other at the same time, it's almost a spiritual state—and therefore easily lost in the torrent of life. You try to get it again, but it's lost, and can only be approximated. Pleasure. Sex. Entertainment. But it finds you again, in art, in music, in a sunset—it catches you off guard. You can't plan it. But there you are. And that's all—it penetrates straight to you and you're released again. And that's what paradise is. It's not a place, really, it's a state of mind."

She paused several seconds, thinking of what she had said so far, then continued. "Beauty—that is, real beauty that inspires an aesthetic experience, an enchantment of the heart—that beauty is a reminder to us that there's some harmony in all this dissonance, that there's something divine about life, that there's something lovable about it. And that behind all this," she made a short sweeping motion with her hand, "is something clean and pure and sensitive."

The force and determination left her voice, and she became gentle and sympathetic, almost sad. "So you don't burn poems that serve as reminders of that state of mind."

Elizabeth sat motionless and silent for several moments staring at the candle flame. Then she looked around the room, as if trying to absorb it into her memory. It looked much the same as when she crawled into it: the marked books, the cluttered desk, the half-visible stereo. She stood up, stretched and walked to the door. David's heart began beating hard. "Where are you going?" he blurted before he could stop himself.

She turned around with her hand on the door. She pulled it open slowly, and then looked at him. The light in the hall poured in over her shoulder. He could see the color of her hair, now highlighted by the hall lamp, the deep red of her lips, the satiny quality to her dress.

"We have got a date. You know—me and you. Us. You're taking me dancing to redeem yourself. So hurry up and get shaved and dressed." She pulled the door behind her, saying, "You're not getting away so easily this time."

David stayed on the bed, staring at the ceiling, not thinking or analyzing, just feeling an incandescent connection to the apparition of Elizabeth that had just been in the room. He began to feel radiant and larger than his body. The glow in her eyes, her laugh, her eccentricity, her dingy ideas now seemed to fit into one seamless image. Then he got up and walked into the bathroom. He flicked the light on and began humming "Shall We Dance?" as he started washing up.

*David and Elizabeth
at Mrs. Spade's*

SOME evenings, like this evening, the three of them gravitated around Melinda's couch and large, oval coffee table. Melinda did not mind; she liked the company. David and Elizabeth liked visiting. David sat leisurely spread over her couch, and Elizabeth sat Indian-style leaning into the shoulder of David's outspread arm.

"Like a beer?" Melinda offered.

"Oh, I dunno, Sam—whatcha got?" David asked, using the nickname Elizabeth had pinned on Melinda.

"Millers."

"That sounds fine."

"You want anything, Liz?"

"No—you know I can't drink too much of that stuff without having a night rampant with live action thrillers for dreams. It only takes a slight jar for my mind to start running amok—then I spend the whole night racing from one dream through another and wake up exhausted."

"Oh, come on," Melinda said.

"No, I—"

"Come on!"

"All right already! You win."

"Good!" Melinda said. She sprang up to go to the kitchen. There was nothing she liked better than getting Elizabeth drunk.

As soon as she walked through the kitchen door, Elizabeth gave David a quick kiss on the cheek. David returned the peck and brushed some of her long auburn hair away from her eyes. She stuck her tongue out at him and pulled the hair back where it had been. David adroitly changed the subject and commented on the decor of Melinda's living room. He said he liked it. Elizabeth agreed, though in fact it was much too simply decorated for her taste, almost barren.

The beige walls matched the beige sofa and chairs. The carpet was dark gray, almost black, and made the couch and chairs look as if they were floating in space. The marble coffee table between the chairs and sofa was like a pale brown cloud they could rest their feet on, and over their heads was the shade of a large, silver vault lamp whose base was well over ten feet away in the corner. Melinda had some of Liz's paintings on the walls above her well-stocked book cases. It was a large room that seemed uncluttered and spacious.

Melinda returned from the kitchen with a tray full of glasses, pretzels, potato chips and beers. She carefully placed the tray on the coffee table, then handed out the glasses. As she handed Liz her glass, she said, "I don't know why you always put me through that routine when you know all along you're absolutely craving one, darling."

"Well, truth be known," Elizabeth countered, "I've never seen anyone's eyes light up with so much enthusiasm as when you offer me a beer—it's practically demonic. What is this mysterious pleasure you get out of my inebriation?"

"She's just trying to open up the channels of communication," David said.

"As if I don't yap enough already—I'm one of the few extant sufferers of diarrhea of the mouth left in this part of the country. She doesn't have to ply me—"

"Now let's be fair to Melinda," David interjected. "After all, it is her couch and coffee table we're gravitating around this evening. She's just trying to create a basis of common understanding upon which to establish a fruitful conversation."

"Oh, isn't he cute?" Liz sneered to Melinda.

"Yeah, and you love it, too," Melinda sneered back.

"Now girls—*girls*, behave yourselves. Elizabeth, here's your beer. Melinda, here's yours. Drink some basis of common understanding and let's yap decently and civilly about something."

"Oh, Liz!" Melinda said. "I painted my nails this morning—aren't they charming?" She held her nails up for Liz to see. They were painted a bright, light green.

"Yesss," Liz vamped, "you have an absolutely vapid taste in nail polish—I'm chartreuse with envy."

"Really, darling—you really think so? I saw this color on some femme fatale in a dream I had the other night and simply *had* to have it."

"Really?" Elizabeth asked with a sudden genuine interest. "You dream with that much detail?"

"Always."

"Me, too!"

"Me, too," David added. "I've had some really unusual ones."

"Oh, yeah? Like what?" Elizabeth asked, assuming a sort of analytical curiosity.

"Well, once when I was about seven or eight—"

"Hm-hmm."

"I was staying over night at my friend Michael Siegel's house—"

"Oh, I see."

"He was Jewish."

"Ahh."

"Come on, Liz, let me finish my story."

"Oh, OK."

"Well," David shot a sly glance at Elizabeth, "I dreamed that I woke up in the middle of the night to go to the bathroom. Maybe I sleep-walked. I was all dazed and sleepy, stumbling down the hall with my eyes barely open, bumping into things, and just before I got to the bathroom, I saw this angelic perfect being at the end of the hall, about six feet tall. I wasn't amazed or startled or anything like that. But there was this radiant being with a glowing nimbus and all, you know, and, uh—I just accepted him right there. I don't know how long we stood there—there seemed to be some telepathic rapport, some sort of exchange, but most of it was way over my head. At any rate, after a bit, I remembered I was thirsty, so I started to go in the bathroom, and I asked him if he wanted a drink, too. He sort of emanated 'no,' so I went in, and when I came out, he was gone."

"So then what happened?" Melinda asked.

"Well, then I went back to bed and forgot all about it till I read *Frannie and Zooey*, you know, and you know what? Salinger describes a similar dream, or something, so then I remembered this amazing dream and it's stuck with me—this image of an angel at the end of the hall at Michael Siegel's house. Amazing, isn't it?"

"Jeez—yeah, that's great," Melinda agreed.

"What'd he look like?" Elizabeth asked.

"Well, it's hard to say. Luminous . . . I can't remember what the details of his face were—dark eyebrows, no beard. He was at the end of the hall, so—"

"Definitely masculine?"

"Yeah. I had this impression of beauty and a brilliant, glowing whiteness to his robes, and this unlimited compassion and love, but not in a syrupy religious or pious way—just unencumbered by anything else. But other than that, I don't remember exactly. It was very vivid and three-dimensional and detailed, more detailed than my seven- or eight-year-old imagination was capable of then."

"So you think it was real?" Melinda asked.

"Oh, no—just that it's incredible how much detail and brilliance the mind is capable of even at that age."

"Well, you know what?" Melinda said.

"No, what?" Elizabeth teased.

"I have these detailed dreams, too, but they're only in snatches—"

"Snatches?" Elizabeth repeated.

"Little *flashes*—like this gorgeous woman walking through a party and the most attractive man in the room noticing her as she passes through the groups of conversations. The dream is just that moment of her passing through and being noticed. And the thing is, I wake up with this poignant feeling of having been through some intensely moving experience, and all that I remember is this little moment, the flash—and the color of her nails. I don't know what to make of it."

"You're probably—" David began, but was interrupted by the telephone ringing. Melinda grimaced and rolled her eyes towards the ceiling.

"That goddamn phone—I oughta take it off the hook when you two come over." She got up to go answer the phone in the kitchen.

David also got up and walked over to look out the window. Melinda's "Hello" and phone conversation were muffled, but could almost be pieced together.

After a few moments and a clearly audible "I thought I told you," Elizabeth stated, "It's her ex."

David muttered, "Hm-hmm." His attention had wandered to the bookshelves, and being an incorrigible personal library snoop, he was giving Melinda's bookshelves a thorough perusal. He, like all other bookshelf inspectors, expected to divine some special insight into the owner's psyche by the selection and arrangement of her books. He had already inspected Melinda's library several times on previous visits and was by now more than superficially familiar with her preference for pre-World War II authors like Colette, Woolf, Fitzgerald, and Toomer; her peculiar placement of the Bible next to Kafka and Ayn Rand on a bottom shelf; the collection of Hesse and Mann interrupted by Ian Fleming's James Bond series; and the film books mingled with Shakespeare and Moliere.

As he pulled out a copy of *Le Mort d'Arthur*, Elizabeth informed him that Melinda was not going to get her alimony that week and that she was absolutely livid over it. David asked her if she had read *Le Mort d'Arthur*. She said no, and neither had Melinda, probably. He told her that she ought to read it; there were some very touching stories about Christian feudal myth and the Holy Grail.

Before Elizabeth could comment, Melinda abruptly re-entered the room, swearing, "Sonofabitch!"

"What happened?" Elizabeth asked.

"You know very well what happened, elephant ears—Jack's gonna be late on the payments again. Honestly, I don't know why I still tolerate that guy, sometimes. Too horny, I guess. Well, where were we?"

"Maybe you should take him to court or something," Elizabeth suggested.

"Nah, it's not that serious," Melinda answered. "And besides, I need the attention sometimes, so late alimony is something I'll just have to learn to live with, goddamn it. So, where were we?"

"You're not too upset or anything, are you?" David asked, still standing near the bookshelf.

"No—no. I'm all right. Just fine. If anything, I was upset by the interruption. It was just starting to get interesting. Where were we?"

"Dreams. Detailed dreams," Elizabeth answered.

"Oh, yeah." She turned to David. "You were going to say something about my short subject dreams."

"Uh, right," David replied absent-mindedly. "Something about you're only waking up with the tip of the iceberg and forgetting the rest, but getting the intensity of all of the dream concentrated into the vignette, or something like that."

"Oh . . . yeah, maybe," Melinda said as if she had expected something else. The conversation lapsed into silence for a few minutes while their minds drifted in different directions.

David started to wander back to the couch, but Melinda, seeing that he was near the front door, said, "Oh! Could you put the porch light on while you're up? Tonight's my night to pay the paper boy. Lord knows why I keep getting the damn thing—I never read it."

"For the movie schedules," Elizabeth reminded her.

"Oh, yeah. Right."

David flipped two or three switches on and off until he found the porch light. Then he walked back to the couch with the copy of *Le Mort d'Arthur* in his hand and sat down. He leafed through the pages for ten or fifteen minutes while Melinda and Elizabeth talked about foreign films with the subtitles versus the dubbed-in ones. Soon they had each polished off their first beers and Melinda left to get some more.

When she came back, David held up the book and asked, "Have you read this?"

"Well . . . sorta." Melinda winced.

"Whaddya mean 'sorta'?"

"Well-l . . . I sorta read the good parts and skipped the rest. I saw the movie—"

"Camelot?" Elizabeth asked. "The one with Peter O'Toole and Vanessa Redgrave?"

"Yeah, that's the one. I saw that and wanted to get some more of the chivalry and romance, so I picked up the book. My Middle English is rusty, so I read the parts I could, and skipped the rest. Why'dja ask?"

"Oh, I saw it over in your bookshelves and—" David's face brightened. "Oh, now I remember what I was going to say before—"

"About what?" Elizabeth asked.

"About her short dreams—"

"I know. They're in Middle English so she only remembers the parts she can translate, right?" Liz suggested.

"That's an interesting idea," David pondered, "that if you dream in a foreign language, naturally you'd be less inclined to remember it—but, no, that's not what I was thinking. I was thinking it's important to sort of investigate the mood you wake up in in order to glean more info out of your dreams."

"And by what feat of mental gymnastics did you flip from there to *Le Mort d'Arthur*?" Elizabeth asked.

David turned to Melinda and said, "Isn't Liz cute?"

"As a bug's ear," Melinda answered.

Elizabeth snorted with mock indignation.

"Well, as I was saying," David paused to look at Elizabeth, "before I was so *rudely* interrupted, I was thinking you need to review the dreams while you're still more or less intimately involved with them. And then," he paused to look at Elizabeth again, "while I was thinking about this, I saw *Le Mort d'Arthur* and I remembered another dream I had—"

"About knights, right?" Elizabeth asked.

"No. This one was actually a very unusual sort of dream. I just had it recently—and it was so real.

"I dreamed I was with this group of people and we were sitting in a circle—this is what *The Morte Darthur* reminded me of, the round table and all."

Elizabeth noticed that he was beginning to get really interested in the conversation for the first time that evening. She watched his eyes flashing as he began describing the dream. He sat up and started darting his hands around to emphasize what he was saying.

"Well, at any rate, we were sitting in a circle, about eight or ten of us, and it was very warm and the air had a gold quality about it. We didn't seem to be saying anything, but were experiencing each other—the ineffable pleasure of touching souls. All of us at once. We weren't really bodies, but we weren't really without them, either. Some were femalish. Some were male-ish. It was very beautiful. The purity of the communication—it was like I was right in their minds and they were right in mine—nothing in between. Well, I don't know how to describe it, the presence, the sensitivity. They were all very happy to have me with them. It seemed to last for ages, but with no time passing by.

"And then . . . well, this . . . uh . . . this big, black, spiraling tunnel started sucking me up. It was pulling me and I couldn't stop it. It was this time, this universe . . . this life pulling on me to come back—time to go back, time to go back to my body and be in this place.

"Then I was sucked up by this black funnel thing—it was sort of like I was a two dimensional poster of myself and was torn away from this circle of people swirling and twisting away above them and the last thing I saw was one of their hands reaching up in the tunnel trying to bring me back . . . but there I was, being pulled up feet-first with my arms stretched out below me, straining to reach this being's fingertips. Just that last moment of seeing our fingertips inches apart as I was swirled away.

"And then I woke up instantly—like right then—with my arm stretched out above me and this . . . this paradise-lost sort of sorrow in my chest. It was the strangest thing."

"That was a dream?" Melinda asked.

"Hm-hmm." David nodded his head and shrugged, as if it were out of his hands, it simply happened and he was reporting the event as it occurred as objectively as possible.

Melinda tacitly accepted the implication of the shrug. Satisfied that he was not manufacturing a story simply to tease, she shook her head and muttered, "Gyod."

At moments like this, Elizabeth's mind frequently fell upon peculiar details, like this nonverbal exchange of doubt, reassurance and acceptance between David and Melinda. She sat silent, appearing to be enchanted by the implications of the dream, while in actual fact she was silently amused by their brief use of sign language to impart a somewhat complex communication. She seemed to be viewing them through a soundproof glass booth. Suddenly aware of this gulf between their conception of her silence and the actual, she made an effort to recollect David's dream as much as possible. As she reviewed David's telling of the dream, another wave of unaccustomed sensations swept over her. A warm, sensual feeling swept over her body, emanating from her thighs—she was suddenly unmistakably sexually aroused. She moved closer to David and pulled his arm around her, curling her feet up underneath her. Conscious again of the disparity between David and Melinda's state of mind and hers, she made another effort to harmonize with their mood. She marveled at the idea that in the space of a few moments she had been attentive, then clinically, but obtusely, observant, and then sexually aroused.

In the same strain of thought, she asked David, "Were you sexually attracted to any of them—you know, like was it sort of an intense sexual-type pleasure?"

David wrinkled his brow and, smiling, asked, "And by what feat of mental gymnastics did you leap from my metaphysical dream to sex?"

"Metaphysics always makes me horny, honey, you know that," she said.

"Must be a soldered connection between intense physical pleasure and intense spiritual pleasure in her switchboards," Melinda commented.

"Don't make fun of my switchboards, Miz Spade—your switchboards have the same sordid hotline—it's our major point in common upon which we've based our entire relationship. You're treading on sacred ground!"

"You may have a point there, sweetheart, but—"

"Christ! Come on, you two. Here we are, knights of Sam's round table making limited forays into the dark recesses of mystical consciousness and you two sit bickering about—"

"We're not bickering. If you'd been paying any attention at all, you would've seen we were finished bickering, weren't we, Sam?"

"Hm-hmm."

"So m.y.o.b." Elizabeth pretended to pout.

After several moments, David sighed. Staring at the marble surface of the coffee table, he said, "Sometimes I feel within inches of a piece of truth—a penetrating insight. I feel like I'm almost in the center of some immense personal and cultural condition—I'm almost ready to see it clearly for the first time, resolve the confusion into its true light—and then . . ."

"And then what?" Elizabeth asked, trying to feel out if he might really be upset.

"I get distracted. I get hungry or the phone rings or I suddenly notice I'm cold and have to turn the heat up. And then the whole logical framework I was following is gone—the flow is gone. It's like by accident I happened to wander through the right sections of a vast labyrinth and almost walked right out, but for some reason didn't and then I'm lost because I don't know how to retrace my steps to get back to the way out. Oh, fuck it. These are just words."

Elizabeth glanced at Melinda.

"I get so fed up with words. Words, words, words. We sit around this goddamn coffee table and talk each other's—"

"Whoa there." Elizabeth ran her fingers gently through David's hair. "Wait a second now—what's going on, sweetheart?"

"I'm getting tired of two-dimensional, kinetic thought. Give me some visions, some divine apparitions—you know what I mean? Things are looking goddamned flat and just when we're about to come upon something interesting you're not even listening. And if you can't stick—I get all caught up in you're not listening so maybe it's not so important or—oh, hell, I don't know, but the thing is shattered now. We may as well just get drunk and watch TV. I feel like we're just spewing a lot of verbal pollution into the air."

"Well look—uh— you're right, sort of. I was listening, but then I got wrapped up in the way you were talking—not what you were talking about—I was listening, but I wasn't paying attention." She winced. "Well, I mean I was listening, but I wasn't listening to your train of thought, exactly." She winced again. "Oh, hell . . . maybe you're right—let's get drunk and see if there's any rowdy nonsense on the tube." The three of them sat motionless for a few minutes. "I'm sorry. I just wasn't feeling metaphysical."

"Oh, it's not your fault, Liz," David said reassuringly.

"It really comes down to my concentration. I get distracted too easily by little things and miss the big ones. So, big deal. Those are the breaks. There really isn't that much to say about these screwball dreams. They happen and there's something significant about them, but damned if I understand what the hell's going on. Fuck 'em."

Melinda was upset. A weak depression welled up within her, and she felt helpless to salvage the conversation and the evening.

"Look, you two. I happen to still be interested."

"No, that's all right. I'm just going to go home and read for a while. You guys finish off the beers, OK?" He got up and started for the door. Elizabeth and Melinda followed him together. Melinda stroked the back of Elizabeth's head and let her hand fall to rest on her shoulder.

Elizabeth smiled at her and walked up to David. She kissed him on the lips. "I'll come by later," she whispered.

"OK, Liz." He looked over to Melinda. "Bye, Sam. Make sure there ain't none a' them beers left—you hear?"

"Yassir, Mastuh David. Bye-bye."

David shut the door behind him. He felt the crisp evening air press against him. There was a stale taste in his mouth and an aching sadness in his chest. He took a few deep breaths and absorbed the mood of the neighborhood—quiet, dark, and yet everything seemed to have sharp outlines, a certain visual clarity that countered, then filtered through his muddled state of mind. Feeling lighter, he half-skipped down the porch steps and walked briskly to the sidewalk. From next door, a boy with a book of receipt stubs ran past him and up Melinda's walk. David turned, and through the living room window, saw Melinda and Elizabeth with their feet propped up on the coffee table, the silver lamp pouring yellow light over them as they became deeply engaged in another conversation.

A Quartet in Limbo

I

CHRISTOPHER STARED OUT THE WINDOW of his third floor
office watching white clouds brush against the brown and green
stubble covering Hollywood's hills. There were certain points
of any day when he did not care about keeping his job, paying
the rent or anything really. At those moments, he turned to his
window, subliminally listening to the radio as he submitted to
a sort of psychological entropy that ebbed through his mind,
disintegrating whatever it touched.

His eyes drifted over the parking lot of Dar Magreb's Middle
East restaurant to the hazy silhouettes of trees and bushes following the spine of the hills. He saw purple-bloomed trees,
different palms and unusual shrubbery which he referred to
as natural radiation mutants. He wondered what their names
were.

For a moment, one of the hills appeared to move like a
giant iguana shifting listlessly in its sleep. The clouds swelled
into dense masses of black and silver spreading across a dark
green sky. Another hill seemed to prepare itself to pounce.
Christopher slipped effortlessly into the vision of two immense
beasts bursting up from their slumber, gnashing their teeth,
biting toes, ribs and shoulders, their entrails spilling through
the serene canyons, smashing homes in the blood-soaked
carnage.

The illusion ended as abruptly as it began, leaving Christopher with an amused enchantment over its bizarre intensity.
His eyes wandered down the street to below his window, and
he imagined a series of three paintings, a triptych, depict-
ing what he had envisioned. He was making a mental note

to draw a sketch of them at home when a tall, slender girl, about twenty-four years old, slipped into his office clutching a clipboard to her chest. She waited a few moments before saying anything, shifting her weight from one leg to the other. Her blond hair was pulled back tight into a bun, exaggerating the length of her neck and the size of her dark brown eyes, giving her the look of a plaintive, Scandinavian orphan.

"Christopher?" she finally asked in a firm, businesslike voice.

Christopher continued staring out the window, watching a hooker get out of a dark brown Bentley. The girl imagined Christopher's face behind the dense mass of matted, curly hair, wondering whether his deep-set eyes were closed or were squinting into the distance. His sharp, angular features always reminded her of some species of bird, but she could never decide which one. She pursed her lips in exasperation.

"Christopher?"

Startled, Christopher swung his chair around to see who had interrupted his musing. He saw the girl and smiled.

"Oh, hi Annie. What's up?" he said distantly, but affectionately.

"You're going to have to stop being so absent-minded,"

Christopher grimaced. He knew what was coming: it was the end of the week, and the job was getting to her.

"I was just in Elaine's office and she's bitching about your projects all being late. You guys don't take her seriously, but she's making a federal case out of it and you're in here staring out the window looking down whores' blouses."

Christopher cocked his head to the side. "How'd you know that?"

Anne did not reply. Christopher leaned forward and studied her face. "You know, Anne, you look really nice today—whadja do?" Anne glared out the window. "Let's see . . . you put rouge on for a change—"

"Christopher—"

"No, maybe you just changed the color of your eye shadow. It seems to match your eyes better—"

"Christopher—" Anne cooed with a false motherly lilt, letting the clipboard slip to her side as she stared towards Christopher's desk.

"And you've got on one of those sheer, push-up bras—"

"Christopher!"

"And that silky blouse clinging—" Christopher ducked as the clipboard slammed into the top of his chair, its papers flying loose then shooting off in various directions.

"Christopher, will you shut the fuck up and listen!"

Christopher leaned over, picked up the clipboard and began neatly replacing the scattered pages.

"Annie, how can I listen when you're so luscious that my mind becomes unidimensional?"

"Buddy, you've got nothing but a one track mind, under any circumstances."

"Oh, I wouldn't say that." Christopher snapped the papers into place. "Sometimes I think about growing up and becoming a rock 'n' roll star."

"Yeah, well, you better do some quick growing up or learn to like the spaghetti and bean sprouts diet you'll be on if you get fired."

"Annie, Annie, Annie. What would I do without you?"

"You'd just flirt with someone else."

"And there you'd be, attention-starved, collapsed behind a row of shot glasses, trying to drown your sorrows with the heart of the agave plant, suffering DT's before you reach thirty, your liver hanging in your gut like a phlegm-sodden combination burrito—"

Annie bent forward with one hand on her stomach.

"Ugh—Christ, lemme out of here—I think I made a wrong turn and ended up in Ward C of Camarillo." She edged toward the door, pretending to be worried he would jump the moment she turned her back.

"Yeah, well, it was nice talking to you," Christopher said politely.

Anne opened the door and sneered.

"Bye," Christopher said. "And tell that Mongoloid bitch Elaine that if she has any complaints about my goddamn work to see me about it 'cause as far as I know I'm putting out just as much as anyone else and we're ahead of schedule and I don't like backstabbers that spread malicious rumors about people because they don't think and act like little do-bees or trained seals."

Anne whispered, "Shhh!" and jerked the door shut.

Christopher liked Anne. She was bright, conscientious and pretty. She nine-to-fived to support herself and was also in something of a quandary about what to do with her life. They had spent many lunches and afternoons being sounding boards for each others ideas, trying to justify working instead of being starving artists. She had a pretty good sense of humor when she was not being moody. After work, they returned to their respective apartments and she pretended to write and he pretended to paint.

Christopher shifted his chair toward his desk. He looked over his computer printout of the project schedule and found that two of his projects were indeed late. He wrinkled his mouth self-disparagingly, shook his head and sighed.

"Well, how about that!" he said aloud. "Son of a bitch."

He pulled a folder off a shelf and opened it on his desk. Yawning, he began collating the pages of a report. Soon the assorted pages were strewn in front of him. His job as an editor for an audience studies company required a meticulous detail orientation that he was only capable of enduring in short spurts, which he alternated with bouts of playful banter with his office mate, Larry, staring out the window, or flirting.

After forty minutes of diligent concentration, Christopher looked up and wondered where the hell Larry was; he had been out of the office for over an hour. For about a month it had seemed like Larry had been spending a lot of time out of the office, not because he had things to do out of it, but because he was avoiding being in it. Christopher could not put his finger on it but was almost to the point of asking Larry directly if he was upset with him over something. Christopher walked over to Larry's empty chair, and seeing a six-commercial project piled on his desk, realized that he was probably just timing the commercials' scripts.

He stood at the desk, tapping a pen absent-mindedly, then quickly grabbed a sheet of paper and wrote in a feminine script:
"Larry, dear—where've
you been? I need a
massage & I've been here
3 times and left 3 times
unsatisfied . . . yr dove,
A."

CHRISTOPHER left the note prominently in the middle of Larry's papers and returned to his own desk. Several minutes passed without Larry's returning and Christopher's attention wandered to the radio above his shoulder. He raised an eyebrow, then grabbed the radio off the shelf and started switching the station toward the end of the dial.

A minute of work rarely passed without Christopher having his radio turned on. For months it had been the disciplinary executives', especially Elaine's, complaint with Christopher. They claimed it distracted him. He countered that he needed it to stay awake. They still objected, asserting that the radio agitated the adrenal glands of those near it, as it was usually at the center of any rowdiness that broke out on the floor. They thought it was too noisy for a professional business atmosphere. Anytime a project went out with an error, Elaine would forbid the playing of the radio, which Christopher would obey for an afternoon or two, then would proceed to ignore. The professional silence broken by the noise of pens scratching across papers, pages of reports shuffling in the distance and an occasional phone ringing, drove Christopher into mind-fogged spells of unconsciousness. The trenchant, offbeat music of his favorite radio station gave his mind the edge it needed to conquer the incipient sleepiness waiting to ebb through his veins at any point of the day.

While Christopher was engrossed with adjusting the tuning and volume, the door opened quietly and Larry snuck in. He was a tall, olive-complexioned son of a Jewish mother and an Episcopalian priest. His big, wide-spaced green eyes, curly hair, and gangling mannerisms had once prompted Christopher to accuse Larry of having been sired by a St. Bernard. Larry did not deny it except to say, "It must have been one hell of a brilliant mutt to propagate someone with a brain as massive as mine."

He was wearing a banana-colored t-shirt, turquoise pants that just covered his ankles, and red tennis shoes that looked like he had worn them to run through oil spills on the beach. Standing in the doorway with an impish glint in his eye, he looked more like an escapee from a carnival act than a Princeton graduate apprenticing as an editor on the way to becoming an account executive.

After staring at Christopher a few moments, he said, "You spend more time playing with that goddamn radio than you spend playing with your moth-eaten penis."

Christopher jerked his head up to see Larry standing at his desk. "Did you change the station, you phlegm-sodden spinach brain?" Christopher jeered.

"Christ, did I do the world a favor when I taught you to speak "phlegm-sodden"? If it weren't for my immense brain's capacity to generate new figures of speech, I'd resent your parasiting off my metaphors."

"If I remember correctly," Christopher said, "it was originally 'as mucous infested' which you plagiarized off me to get 'phlegm-sodden.' "

"You remember *in*correctly. It started with 'as appetizing as regurgitated worm entrails' which you euphemized into 'mucous infested' which in turn evolved into "phlegm-sodden.'"

"Oh yeah. Right. I forgot all about that. So, did you change the station, or what?"

"Yeah." Larry leaned over his desk and flipped through his calendar. "I got tired of listening to Daryl Wayne complaining about disco's debilitating beat—if he doesn't like it, he should just smash the record against the table, scratch glass, then forget about it. He's starting to sound like an 80-year-old woman complaining about her arthritic clitoris."

Larry picked up the note on his desk and Christopher continued talking while pretending to resume work on the proofreading project spread in front of him.

"Yeah, well you didn't have to change it to the Jehovah's Witness station. I thought I was listening to a Bach festival until Reverent Jehovah—"

"What the hell is this?" Larry demanded, holding the note.

"Oh," Christopher glanced at Larry's outstretched hand, uncapped some Liquid Paper and proceeded to brush a few words away. "Annie was in here a couple of times looking for you."

"Well, 'bye! If Elaine comes looking for me, tell her I'm at the clinic getting a VD check," Larry said as he lunged toward the door.

"Sure, I can do that," Christopher replied in a syrupy voice.

Larry smirked lustfully and shut the door behind him. Christopher's upper lip curled into a half-smile as he continued brushing white-out over typographical errors.

Within a few minutes, the door swung open and banged against the wall. Larry and Anne charged into the room like a couple of detectives breaking into a criminal's hideout.

Christopher glanced up from his report. "Sure, come on in, have a seat. Can I help you?"

"All right, you degenerate progeny of a syphilitic monkey—"

"Now wait a minute, Lar," Anne interrupted sweetly, "let's not jump to any hasty conclusions." She walked over behind Christopher and put her arm around his shoulder. "Let's look this over objectively—"

"Naw—" Larry picked up his X-acto knife and gave it a couple of test throws into his desk. "Let's just rip him to shreds and feed him to the pigeons. They're dumb enough to—"

"Now Lawrence—what we're dealing with here is the stifled creative impulse of a fledgling genius—"

"Assholes stop being fledglings after they're twenty-five, and aberrant behavior doesn't qualify maladjusted social deviants for any mental capacity awards."

"I understand what you're saying, Lawrence," Anne said, "but what I'm trying to say is that what we've got here is a sensitive and intelligent individual," Christopher nodding his head in affirmation, "forced by the exigencies of rent, food and his weekly fix of movies to prostitute himself, to sell out, to the flat tedium of the nine-to-five, helping IBM, Universal or Play-Tex keep their fingers on the pulse of America's psyche, his mind chained to the trivial, his spark spent on the petty, his blunted imagination driven to vicarious releases—"

"Sounds like a kind of masturbation to me," Larry said in a rural drawl.

A smile started to crack across Anne's face which she could not quite suppress, but before it did, the door suddenly swung open again, and Dale, their supervisor, walked in.

She was a plain-featured girl, her face a little too broad, her nose a little too flat, her hips a little too chunky to be considered pretty. Larry had once commented that if not for her large chest and meticulous make-up work, she'd be "pressing the periphery of abject unattractiveness, the end of the line for her gene pool." Dale stood tight-lipped and silent in the doorway, letting her supervisory presence dampen the aura of levity.

After a few moments she said, "Elaine wants the socializing cut to a minimum—one of the board members apparently made a remark about the loose atmosphere up here after seeing you—" she looked at Anne "—and Christopher tickling each other in the elevator. Elaine has somehow drawn a connection between that and," she looked at Christopher, "two of your projects coming up late on the status report. All I want is the work done on schedule and her off my back. I don't care what you do beyond that. However, she takes it as a personal failure as an executive to receive comments like that and gets mad. So mind your p's and q's for a few days till her temper settles, ok?"

"Sure," the three of them muttered.

Dale said "Thanks" and pulled the door shut behind her.

For a few seconds, Christopher, Anne and Larry stared at the door as if to make sure it was not about to pop open again. Anne started absent-mindedly running her fingers through Christopher's hair.

"Well la-de-da," Larry said in a mixed tone of amusement and hostility.

"I guess we'll have to take the circus out of town for a few days, eh, sports?" Christopher suggested.

"Not if you'd get your reports out on schedule," Anne said, walking over to Larry's desk. "It's hard enough putting up with this nine-to-five crap and going home too washed-out to write or whatever, but when you add to it this constant monitoring of our behavior like we're—the least you could do is follow the goddamn schedule so they don't have an excuse to dominate us."

Both Larry and Christopher knew better than to try to interrupt her—she was not really angry yet, but any slight peep out of them would have set her off on one of her electric fire and brimstone tirades that would have reached critical mass and exploded before they had a chance to blink.

"Oh, quit looking at me like a couple of guiltless schoolboys trying to look guilty. Quite frankly, you two piss me off. You seem to thrive on being on their shit lists. It's like you need the challenge of working under the stress or something. Or maybe it's your way of broadcasting you haven't bought their game—you're here, but you're not part of it, or I don't know. But, at any rate, I don't thrive on it. It's bad enough knowing I'm wasting the best part of my day correcting grammar on market research reports—god, can you believe this—market research reports—it's degrading—just to pay the goddamn rent. I go home and it's like I get a daily prefrontal lobotomy and I spend the rest of the evening reconstructing my missing lobes. And then to have to contend with knowing I'm on their shit lists—it's too much. I end up watching television or going to bed . . .

"It's not your fault, I know that, but you'd be doing me a favor by giving me the security of being able to think, 'Yeah, but at least we get our work done' or 'at least we're on schedule,' or something. It's such a little thing, an easy thing, to do to prevent wasting valuable energy on worrying about losing our jobs, you know what I mean?"

They nodded, muttering, "Uh-huh."

"Well, that's all I have to say. Here endeth the epistle."

"Yeah, ok, Anne. We'll do the best we can," Larry said empathetically. He seemed to enjoy these lectures as signs of Anne's vitality or spunk. Christopher viewed them and her frequent depressions as self-indulgent overreacting, something he had to tolerate until her mood changed.

"OK—I'll try to avoid going off schedule. It's an added aggravation that we don't need. I don't think it's, uh . . ." Christopher stared at his desk a few moments. "Oh, never mind."

"No, go ahead—what is it?" Anne prodded, her anger conspicuously dissolved.

"Oh, nothing," Christopher replied diffidently.

"Sure?"

"Yeah."

"OK. So whaddya wanna do for lunch?"

"Oh hell, I hadn't thought about it yet. Is it lunchtime already?"

"In about half an hour," Anne said as she moved over to Christopher's desk again.

"So where do you want to go?" Christopher asked.

Larry turned away from his desk and started throwing his X-acto knife into the wall. After two or three good shots, he asked, "How about Lou's Quickie?"

"Fine with me," Christopher answered.

Anne picked up Christopher's X-acto knife and began tossing it into the blotter on his desk. Christopher watched her flipping the knife, noticing again that she was unusually attractive that day. He could not put his finger on it exactly, but she seemed to be more alive, more energetic, her eyes brighter, her skin less pale. A few wisps of her hair had fallen loose onto her neck. From his vantage point, he could see most of her chest as she leaned over his blotter. *Honeydew melons*, he thought to himself. *Well, maybe peaches*, he corrected. He liked her chest and her naturally dark red lips and her large, sensitive eyes. She had moments of real beauty which he noted silently and absorbed.

It was these moments that threw Christopher into a quandary about their relationship. For a few seconds, with her eyes bright and her hair, lips and chest swelling in front of him, he was ready to fall in love with her and let fate take them on its rocky, inevitable course. He saw them kissing and making love, being tender and intimate. But then she turned her head slightly and he saw the creases in her brow, the dark shadows around her eyes, the remnants of her frequent indulgences in self-pity and her clinging to fits of emotional extremes as if they were badges of character uniqueness, a sort of pride in her temper tantrums that made them all the more odious to Christopher. The fragile intimacy he had felt the moment before dissipated like an elusive waft of perfume on a breezy afternoon. As the memory of the feeling faded, he turned to look out the window, his eyes focused on the distant profile of the hills, his mind sinking into a thoughtless oblivion.

2

LOU'S QUICKIE GRILL WAS A TRANSPLANTED New York deli, though Anita, Lou's wife, always insisted it was a "New Joisey joint". It did not matter much to Christopher, Larry or Anne—their collective nostalgia for the East Coast readily absorbed its deli atmosphere with abandon and ignored whatever traces of New Jersey Anita chose to bring to their attention. Situated between a Mercedes-Benz repair shop and a row of small film studios, it had the heterogeneous air of a cross between a truck stop café and a lot-shop for actors, actresses and film crews on break. It was a small, permanently crowded place that seated a maximum of thirty people, though a sign on the wall placed the limit at five hundred. It was offbeat enough for Christopher and his circle of workmates to make it an occasional lunch spot, but too small and noisy for a regular stop. The clanking of the dishes, the hissing of the grill and the din of overcompensating voices made it soon lose its novelty after a few consecutive lunches.

Larry burst in the door first, followed by Christopher, Anne and another friend of theirs, Rick. Anne was squawking about Christopher and Larry's having carried her across the street like a bag of dirty laundry, and Larry was telling her to quit complaining, she was lucky they had not used her to stop the taxi that was running through the intersection. They landed at an empty table in the rear, four mounds of flesh piled like bean bags tossed randomly at the corner, invertebrate chunks of protoplasm flopped at odd angles over the edges of their chairs.

"That was real cute, guys," Anita snapped with a grandmotherly saltiness. "Whaddya do for an encore?" Larry grinned. "Next time leave the tornado outside—Rufus gets tired of cleaning up the messes. Here's your menus. I'll be back in a minute."

The talk quickly changed to food as they each took a menu from her.

"Oh Christ, what am I going to satiate my ravenous appetite with today?" Larry asked as he leered at Anne.

"Get your goddamn eyeballs off my tits," Anne demanded, "they're not on the menu."

"Oh, OK," Larry said with a feigned seriousness.

"What should I get?" Anne asked Christopher.

"Well," Christopher began, "the corned beef is scrumptious—it's warm, moist, juicy and thick—really an immense sandwich, just the right consistency. I wake up in the middle of the night with Lou's Quickie corned beef cravings that last all the way to lunch until I satisfy the urge with the real thing."

"He never learned how to masturbate properly, " Larry confided to Anne, "so his libidinal impulses are peculiarly sublimated."

"Oh, thanks," Anne said curtly with a disgusted frown on her face.

Anne, Rick and Larry continued studying their menus. Christopher had walked in knowing what he wanted: a Mintzburger, medium rare, with cheese and tomatoes. It was a third of a pound of spiced and onioned ground beef on a French roll that, salted, was so delicious that he would nearly inhale the thing whole.

Christopher was sitting against the wall, next to Rick and across from Anne. While waiting for Anita to come back for their orders, he took the opportunity to study his friends and the other customers. Seated at the counter were three or four of the usual tattooed, tee-shirted mechanics or truckers smoking cigarettes and idly drinking coffee. At the table across from them was evidently some sort of executive committee that was visiting the area, perhaps one of the studios. They were nattily dressed, their hair recently styled, all wearing expensive-looking watches. They looked out of place on the gaudy, orange polyethylene chairs, especially compared to the men at the counter. Anita's saltiness must have appeared crass or rude to them, Christopher thought—or maybe they were just slumming. He was putting the lid on their categorization as white, Anglo Saxon Protestant indebted suburbanites that drove sun-roofed European sedans when a girl amongst them burst out laughing with Anita and speaking what sounded like Yiddish. He wrinkled his brow at his misestimation of them and returned his attention to his friends. Rick was looking up and had apparently noticed the same thing, for when their eyes met, Rick said, "Never would have guessed her for a Yid, eh?"

"Nope. She had me hook, line and nose," Christopher answered. "Cosmetic surgery strikes again. What are you getting?"

"A deli omelet and a Dr. Brown's. What about you?"

"Mintzburger."

"God—where the hell'd they get the names for these things?"

"They named them after their grandchildren."

"Yeah? Mintz?"

"Beats me—I guess it's a name." Christopher turned to Larry and Anne. "What are you guys getting?"

"Nicky's combo," Larry replied, "and she's fallen prey to your high pressure sales technique, you charmed her—"

"Irresistible, isn't he?" Anne interjected to Larry.

"Yeah, he should be writing ads for this joint. He seems to have found the link between attitudinal responses and purchase behavior shifts towards the advertised product. Have you ever thought of going into market research? You could make millions."

"Ugh. Don't talk about it, please," Christopher pleaded. "I hate to bring up the office for fear I'll bring up my breakfast, too."

"Hey—that's my career you're talkin' about, bud," Rick pretended to complain.

"Career my ass," Anne replied.

"I could think of better things to do to your ass," Larry said, leaning his head on Anne's shoulder.

"Well, forget 'em. You'll just die a frustrated old man," Anne said. Larry frowned. "And besides, you know my heart belongs to Chrissie."

Anita walked up and slapped her pad of order blanks on the table before Larry could say anything else. "OK, boys and girls, whaddya want?"

"Nicky's Combo and a Hires on the rocks," Larry blurted.

"Corned beef sandwich and milk."

"A deli omelet and creme soda."

"And I want a Mintzburger, medium rare, and a creme soda."

"Cheese and tomatoes?"

"Yep."

"Okey doke. I think I got all that. Now behave yaselves a while till I bring your drinks."

"Okey doke," Larry parroted.

AFTER Anita left, a period of silence lulled between them, the train of the conversation apparently forgotten. Larry studied the men at the counter as they finished off their coffees and cigarettes. Christopher watched Anne as she stared into a space in front of the table. She was slouched deep in her chair, legs stretched out in front of her. Rick fidgeted with his silverware, tapping his spoon on his paper napkin. The random tapping slowly developed into a recognizable rhythm and Christopher asked, "'Panic in Detroit'?"

"Yep," Rick answered. He suddenly changed the rhythm, then asked, "What's this?"

Christopher listened intently, but Rick stopped before he could pick out what he was tapping. "Do it again," he demanded.

"OK." he tapped it out again.

"Ya got Bowie on the brain—that's 'Rebel, Rebel.'"

"My man!" Rick exclaimed. "Whatcha doin' this weekend?"

"Oh, I dunno. Don and I'll probably make a ritual visit to the beach, soak up some sun and get beat around by some waves. Then we'll probably go catch a couple of films. What about you?"

"Bowie's coming to town, so I was gonna catch him over at UCLA."

"How's Donnie?" Anne asked, snapping out of her reverie.

"Fine, I guess," Christopher said, smiling at her sudden shift of attention.

"How's he like Columbia?"

Anita brought a tray with their drinks and began distributing them.

"Well-l," Christopher began, squinting up one side of his face, "he's sort of mixed, I guess. He likes the money and he likes working at a studio—that's what he was trying to do all along, break in and all."

"But . . . ?" Anne led him.

"But it's pretty boring work—compiling Nielsen and Arbitron ratings. And he says everyone's so wrapped up in status stuff, who gets what according to seniority, who gets a walnut desk, who gets the new IBM monitor, who gets coffee delivered first—a lot of petty backstabbing, you know. He said it isn't as much fun as when he was with us. Lord knows he doesn't miss the work, but he does miss all the fooling around and stuff. Hell, if it weren't for you guys, I wouldn't be able to take this nine-to-five bullshit either. He even said sometimes he thinks about coming back."

"No shit—really?" she asked.

"Yeah. That's what he said."

"Well, I hope he doesn't."

"Oh, I don't think he will. He just says it to have something to complain about." Christopher's voice assumed a patronizing tone. "It's simply a manifestation of his dissatisfaction with the social conditions offered to quasi-creative intellectuals. Bound by the crassly commercial and poverty, he meanders through the valley of comfort, fearing no evil, but all the while knowing he's settling for the easy way out."

"Thanks, Professor Graham," Anne smirked, "your speeches are a mirror held to your psyche, your logic incapable of following a linear path of dialogue as it periodically spirals off to unbridled fantasies only to return as if nothing occurred, making our conversations look like a straight line pulled up into little curlicues every once in a while."

"That's very poetic, Annie—did you ever think about becoming a writer?" Christopher asked.

"Oh, suck dead rats," Anne said, closing the conversation.

Anita cocked an eyebrow as she arrived at their table with their lunches balanced on her hands and arms. "Ok, kiddies, here's you lunches."

They plowed into their food, barely pausing to breathe, except to mutter "Mmmm" or "Yum," until they had polished off half of their sandwiches or omelettes. Larry purposely smacked his lips a few times and Anne kicked his foot until he quit. They paused a bit, then began chatting as they picked at the rest of their meals.

"You guys eat like a bunch of Ethiopian refugees," Anne remarked. "Didn't your mothers ever teach you how to eat like civilized human beings?"

"Nope," Larry answered.

"Oh, you're impossible!" Anne said, shaking her head and smiling affectionately in spite of herself.

"D'ja hear that Dale's boyfriend stood her up again?" Christopher asked.

"No, so?" Rick said through a mouthful of omelet.

"Well, she said that's the last straw and she's dumping him. I think that's why she's been on the rag the last couple of days."

"She's on the rag cause you're off schedule, bean brain," Anne stated.

"I'm hardly ever off schedule—and besides, those projects were late getting to me, Dale knows that, so I think there's something else going on."

"Well, if you spent less time concocting practical jokes to play on me and Larry . . ."

"All right, all right," Christopher surrendered, knowing what he was in for if he didn't. "You win."

"Not till I'm done." Anne pointed her fork at Christopher and he raised his right eyebrow cynically. "What would have happened if Elaine walked in and found that note on his desk? Huh? What would have happened? They're looking for places to cut back, you know, and she, in her management-oriented logic, would have viewed it as a rough draft for a resignation. Did you think about that?"

Christopher muttered, "Unh-uh." The look she had just given him set his mind racing. The glint in her eye and her pursed lips transformed in his imagination to a surrealistic portrait of her determined face surrounded by half-formed objects suggesting her dreams and frustrations, an almost angry face in reverie, crowded by muted reds and discolored yellows, trees and bodies, galactic configurations merging into clefts of crystalline spires, blue and green cityscapes, boats and oceans—a multiplicity of spaces and times converging on the canvas to create a moment of psychological now. He made a mental note to do a rough sketch of it when he got home that evening.

Anne continued, saying, "So what were you thinking when you did it?"

Larry shifted in his seat, studying Christopher's face.

"Oh, nothing in particular. I thought it'd be funny, you know," Christopher smiled impishly, "humor being based on pressing against the edge of tact and all."

"Oh, forget it. You're hopeless, too," Anne said, also smiling, her flash of temper apparently dissipated. "Why do I love you, huh? Lord knows you don't deserve it."

"It's probably my unrelenting sense of truth and justice, my virile physique, my aristocratic—"

"No, she's just plain stupid," Larry said flatly. "Did you ever notice that she says 'huh?' a lot?"

"Oh, the hell with both of you!" She turned to Rick, prepared to ignore Christopher and Larry the rest of their lunch. "What do you have to say for yourself, Rick?"

Rick was finishing off the last of his omelet and held a finger up signaling Anne to wait a second till he swallowed. She waited.

"What's this about cutting back? Are we in for another Black Friday, or what?"

"I don't know for sure, but Dale told me that she overheard Elaine hinting that business is going to be slowing down quite a bit for the next couple of months and that they were going to have to start tightening belts a little, looking for ways to save money."

"Roughly translated, mind your p's and q's 'cause they're looking for people to terminate with managerial prejudice," Larry extrapolated.

"Goddamn—isn't it amazing how news spreads around that joint?" Rick asked.

"Yep," Larry continued, "it's like executive shifts in policies that send off little psychic tremors till the quake hits. Anne here is a glorified cockroach that starts hopping up and down before it hits."

"Thanks a lot, beetle brain."

Before they had a chance to start cat fighting, Christopher said, "Yeah, well, there isn't a lot of what could be called discretionary privacy up there."

"You mean there's a lot of big mouths and tiny brains," Larry interpreted.

"Yeah, I guess you could say that," Christopher answered, mimicking a naïve Mr. Rogers.

Anne stared into space a moment. "Well, there are some

things that just don't need to be spread all over the building. And there's so many intersecting sets of friends that it's extremely difficult to keep anything where it belongs."

"Yeah, but they give out so little info on the company's financial stability," Rick explained. "They don't want us to know when they're making huge profits so we won't ask for raises, and they don't want us to know when they might be cutting back so we don't start looking for other jobs."

Christopher leaned his chin into his palm and said, "That's because they know they'll get a mob of people answering any goddamn help wanted ad. As far as they're concerned, we're expendable drones that fill slots on a paper assembly line. We're supposed to be happily buzzing away at our desks and not causing trouble. We're not paid to think, we're paid to be tame worker bees, you know what I mean? We're beneath being informed, so we have to depend on rumors, and that's all there is to it."

"Smart enough to learn the job and dumb enough not to know when to quit," Larry added.

"Yeah, well, maybe you're right—the only good worker is a dumb worker," Anne concluded, throwing her napkin on her plate. "I think it's time to get back, so let's pay up and get the hell out of here."

They each opened their wallets and threw assorted dollar bills on the table, then left in single file. Larry's hand wandered down Anne's back to pinch her bottom, and she punched him in the ribs as they walked out the door.

3

IT WAS ANOTHER BALMY SATURDAY MORNING at the beach. For three summers now, Christopher and Don had been trying to suspend all forms of urban existence and let it blow off over the shimmering ocean to be assimilated by algae and plankton, as if recycling the synthetic processes of life in the city back into the natural elements of the biosphere. Their summers lasted from May to October, and each week, shifting masses of air, fog, and clouds seemed to pay homage to the inviolability of their Saturdays at the beach.

They usually arrived between ten and eleven while the sun was still burning off the early morning fog. The beige, almost white, sand was warm, sending a layer of ripples into the blanket of air just above it. Later, by two or three, it would pass beyond the realm of comfort and become painfully hot, forcing them to hop from place to place like toads tiptoeing across viscous asphalt. But in the late morning, as they arrived with the slight chill of the morning breeze on their bare skin, their feet merged unflinchingly into the soothing warmth, osmosing the granules of quartz and granite between their toes and around their ankles. Don, being a native Californian and connoisseur of beaches, would say, "Christ, this beach gives good sand," as he buried his feet with each step.

Their beach was Santa Monica Beach, about a half mile south of Will Rogers State Beach (also known as "Gay Beach," according to Don) and about two miles north of the Santa Monica Pier (dubbed "Beaner Beach" by Don). It was about a twenty-minute drive from Christopher's apartment in Hollywood. Don always drove so, according to him, they could listen to his tapes of Dan Hicks or English Beat on the way. Christopher suspected it was really because he did not trust Christopher's driving plus he did not care for the old newspapers, tennis balls, junk mail, sand, dirt and beer bottles on the floor of his car.

They had tried out several beaches during Christopher's first summer in Los Angeles. Malibu was interesting, but parking was impossible and the beach was too rocky; the boulders lining the shore provided life-glutted tide pools but made body surfing extremely dangerous. Zuma's waves were too violent, breaking right on the shore, and Christopher had barely escaped with his nose in place after a few waves had crushed his face into the sand. Venice was entertaining with all its street philosophers, comedians, musicians and psychics, but the beach was so dirty that walking through the sand left a film of gray dust on their skin. Manhattan, Hermosa and Sunset were, in their opinion, good beaches, but too far away for weekly trips. So they had settled for Santa Monica Beach, where the waves were not particularly strong, but the sand, water and air seemed cleaner. It was not too crowded, and the crowd, if any, was usually made up of adolescent or post-adolescent beach kids full of sun and sex. Don once summarized the venue by saying, "It gives good breasts."

The two of them were lying north-south, parallel to the shore, to get as much sun as possible while the sun was still rising. Their heads were propped up by identical blue and green striped beach chairs. Don had his hands and feet buried in the sand. Christopher's were carefully placed within the perimeter of his towel as if he were floating on a raft. They looked like they were related, perhaps brothers. Don, like Christopher, had brown, loosely curled hair and deep-set eyes, though his were grayish blue instead of brown. They had similarly shaped bodies: around six feet tall, long arms and legs, chests not much wider than their hips. Don was taller than Christopher by an inch or two, but was beginning to gain weight around his stomach and shoulders, softening the angularity that he and Christopher had once shared. Christopher's sharp, birdlike features and thin physique gave him a distinctly gangling adolescent look. Neither could be considered virile or robust, though lying in the sun with drops of perspiration swelling on their lips, chests and thighs, a sweaty sheen on their brown skin, the two of them radiated an unasserted sexuality, a sultriness, like the waves of heat lingering above the sand, that caught the eye of some of the semi-naked girls walking by.

Through half-closed eyes, Christopher happened to notice a teen-age girl staring into the dark shadow between Don's legs. He pretended not to notice, thinking to himself, I guess they do these things, too, something he had assumed as natural, but had not seen such an overt example of before. The girl's high, firm chest, dimpled derriere, and ripe skin gave her away as too young for Don's taste. But not for me, he thought, not for me.

"I think that girl was looking at me right up the crotch," Don whispered.

"I thought you were asleep."

"I was coasting. So, was she or wasn't she?"

"I'm pretty sure she was. I think she was counting the beads of sweat on your balls."

"Boy, I don't think I've ever seen a girl look at me like that before. I feel like I've just starred in an X-rated European beach film. Dick's Day at the Beach. A Day in the Life of Harry Ream. Frannie and Dickie." Don squinted up his face and said with a Puerto Rican accent, "An' she was a-lookin' right up my shorts!"

"It couldn't have happened to a nicer guy."

"Thanks," Don said with a tinge of sarcasm.

"She was real cute," Christopher twanged like a hillbilly—his Slim Pickens impression.

"Yeah, but young. Real young. I could've got arrested for contributing to the delinquency of a minor."

Christopher rolled over on his stomach. "You hungry yet?"

"No, not really. Let's bake twenty minutes more, OK?"

"OK." Christopher closed his eyes and tried to imagine the scene around him as if he were out of his body. He placed a group of high school girls about ten yards beyond his feet. The light blue life guard station, its peeling paint, about fifteen yards farther. A dark-haired girl in a maroon, one-piece suit that had less material than most bikinis. Six or seven sun-bleached surfers in their rubber suits flirting with four or five musically-voiced surfer girls. The turbulent foam gurgling as the waves curled, then crashed. He turned the sounds into onomatopoeic words, thinking, Sssssh . . . poom! . . . sssssssss . . . He tried to articulate the sound of the waves' breaking, then fanning out across the sand: Ssssh poom! . . . sssss. More of a p-sounding impact than a b-sounding boom, the air caught beneath the crest acting like a kind of drum, a resounding resonance that slapped down on the water, followed by the aspirant hissing of thousands of tiny bubbles popping on the surface as the wave spent itself on the sand. The cobalt blue of the distant ocean merged into the olive shore and became a soothing refrain of echoed sounds, lulling Christopher into a relaxed, sleepy reverie that soon passed into slumber.

How long he had dozed, he was not sure. He awoke with damp curls stuck to his forehead and neck, his shorts and towel soaked with sweat. He squinted at the bright, steaming sand and the silvery sky. The thick-headed weight of lethargy made him dizzy—it was always like this waking up in the hot early afternoon sun. He sat up and stretched, then hunched over to rest his arms and chin on his knees until the dizziness wore off. A few seconds later, Don stretched and sat up, sweat dripping down his forehead and chest, the skin of his face puffy and wrinkled out of place. The ocean was dark blue, almost indigo, with ripples of spangling reflections pulsating across its surface like flickering pools of mercury. They both took deep breaths, absorbing the fresh, salty air, focusing upon its sharpness and wetness that opened ordinarily sealed-off sections of their lungs.

"Feel like cooling off?" Christopher asked sleepily.

"Um . . . yeah," Don sighed. "Yeah, let's go."

They stumbled up from their towels, slightly stiff-jointed, then started shuffling toward the water. After a few steps, the heat seared through their urban calluses and they took off at a sort of running hop, racing into the ancestral sea without stopping to check its temperature, splashing in heedlessly and diving at the first wave.

The cold, roaring water enveloped their bodies in a muffled

pandemonium, stripping off their sand-flecked sweat and lethargy in one liquid gust and carrying it away to be washed up on the shore, forgotten. They broke the surface with an intense and sudden clarity, an abrupt awareness of now—as if every muscle and nerve in their bodies had been jolted from deep apathy to the threshold of exhilaration.

"Goddamn, does this feel good!" Don shouted.

"I think I've just seen God!" Christopher shouted back. Their words had an odd, staccato brevity as they trod water and panted.

Don pointed out to where the larger waves were breaking. "Let's catch some!"

"OK!"

Don rapidly swam the twenty-five or so yards out, and Christopher dawdled behind, inspecting the gold speckles of light, the bits of blue-green algae and the silvery bubbles of air as he swam. The radiant reflections flashed and sparkled in his eyes. He thought about applying to be reincarnated as a dolphin. Don positioned himself in the center of a three- or four-foot wave, threw his arms out over his head and came gushing toward Christopher, half-consumed by the foaming mass of water. Christopher dived under the wave just in time to let it pass over him without carrying him along. When he popped back up, he could see Don near the shore shouting ecstatically about the wave he had just ridden. Christopher trod water, waiting for Don to swim back out before catching a wave himself. After a minute or two, Don swam up shouting, "Christ, what a great wave! Goddamn, the ocean's giving good wave today."

Christopher shouted, "Let me at 'em!"

They swam about fifteen yards farther out and waited for another good wave. The water swelled up and Christopher tried to swim with the swell in order to catch it as it broke, but it somehow dissipated around him before he could catch it. They let a few smaller waves go by, then the ocean swelled up again, a dark wall of water curving and rushing at them.

Don shouted, "All right, here we go!"

They swam hard along the wave's vector to match its velocity as it curled over them. Christopher arched his back, threw his hands out above his head, his stomach acting like a natural surf board catching the curve of the wave, gliding inside its tube of foaming water, racing just outside the crest's reach until it came crashing down on top of him, tossing his body and twisting his back, the roar of tumultuous water beating his ears and shoulders. He was no longer aiming himself, but was projected pell-mell through the crashing wave, completely at its mercy. This was the moment he loved the best, the reckless loss of control as he tumbled and glided toward the shore. He felt like he was flying through a thick, salty cloud whose air currents buffeted him down and up, then sideways, then down again, finally easing him out of its grip as it gently dropped him off near the shore. Christopher angled himself a little against what was left of the wave, pumping it a little to stretch the ride out as far as he could. He coasted another ten feet, then jumped out of the water, his skin and muscles tingling with an invigorated bliss.

"Goddamn, goddamn, goddamn. I sing goddamn was that a good wave!" he yelled out to Don.

Don yelled back something in agreement, but Christopher could not hear it over the surf. He ran splashing over to Don and they both shouted about the wave. Then they swam out to catch another one, but the waves had suddenly died before they got into position again. They rode in a few less exciting ones and decided to go get something to eat instead of spending the rest of the afternoon waiting for the wave, risking starvation or drowning before it came.

They stumbled out of the water, exhausted and out of breath. "I wish—," Don panted, "I wish I could stay here the rest of my life. Not have to go back to work Monday."

"A professional beached whale."

"Yeah."

"Me too."

They walked up to their spot, their feet oblivious to the sand's heat, and began shaking the sand off their towels before drying off. Don flopped down on his towel first, then Christopher.

"I read about this guy, a yogi, who could convert sunlight into food," Christopher said. "He only needed to eat three or four grapes a week. I wish I could do that."

"Yeah, me too. Maybe we could get someone to hook up some solar energy cells to our stomachs."

"Yeah. Then we'd have to go to the beach everyday."

"Yep," Don answered as if punch-drunk.

"Do you think we idle away our creative energies on adolescent fantasies?"

"Nope."

"Good. Whaddya wanna eat?"

"Sourdough burger and pink lemonade."

Christopher stood up. "Ok. Gimme your dough and I'll go get it."

"No, that's ok. I'll go with ya."

"Okey doke, let's hit it."

They slipped on sandals and started off toward the restaurant situated on the east side of the beach. The cliffs of Santa Monica, the edge of the Los Angeles coastal basin, towered over the tiny restaurant. They were sandy, eroded cliffs, lined by miles of palm trees at the top and plunging to the Pacific Coast Highway at the bottom. Beyond the palm trees were rows and rows of expensive looking coastal high-rises, the final resting places of the moderately wealthy waiting to die, homes for the worn cogs of the American business machine, stooped, gray-haired lemmings waiting for their turn to jump into the ocean. Seagulls idled above the trees, circling in the cloudless, smogless sky. "Postcard picturesque," Christopher thought. He wondered what was behind the steely gray windows and the cleverly designed façades. He imagined a postcard of this scene, beautiful in every detail, with a gaunt, hollow-cheeked woman, her white hair scraggly and uncombed, sitting in a wheelchair looking out her picture window at the sea or right at the viewer. The surface hides the suffering, he thought as they approached the restaurant. He smiled to himself grimly. Maybe if I'm a good boy, in fifty years, I can be up there too.

They had to stand in line at the take-out counter. Ahead of them were assorted bleached, bronzed, and golden teen-age girls, some with braces, some slouching to hide their chests, some conspicuously thrusting their chests out, all bored and chatting cattily as they snuck glances at guys in line between the glances the guys had been sneaking at them, quick furtive glances out the sides of their eyes.

"It's not that I hate my job," Don suddenly said, apropos of nothing. "I'm making more money than I ever was and Maggie, that neurotic bitch, bless her heart, has pushed me up for another humongous raise this month. They spend money like it's water."

"Hm-hmm," Christopher muttered. He did not like to talk when the conversation was probably being eavesdropped by bored line-standers.

Don did not care. "It's just that I know something must be wrong if I have to rely on things outside of work to feel like I'm enjoying life. You know what I mean?"

"Uh-huh." Christopher motioned toward the girl behind the counter, who was waiting for Don to order. "Give her our order."

He ordered two sourdough burgers, two lemonades and two bags of chips. "If my job provided excitement and fulfillment, I wouldn't be looking for it elsewhere, would I?"

"No," Christopher answered, "but who ever said jobs were supposed to be exciting and fulfilling?"

"Me and Barbara." Don smiled, showing he was aware of his ludicrous logic. "Her and I—" Christopher winced. He could not believe that someone as bright as Don could graduate from

high school, much less college, still unwittingly dropping gram-
matical bombs like this into his conversations.

"Are you listening to me, boy?"

Christopher nodded obediently.

"Good. We were talking the other day and we decided that
if you're looking elsewhere for enjoyment in life, then you're
in the wrong job."

They were interrupted by the counter girl, who had brought
up their order. They paid her and left. Christopher carried a
cardboard tray of potato chips and burgers; Don carried the
drinks.

When they were about halfway back to their towels, Don
asked, "Do you think I spend too much time complaining
about work?"

"Maybe a little," Christopher said tactfully.

"Yeah, well to be honest, I don't really mind work that
much—I get a lot of attention 'cause I'm about the only sane
guy there that isn't gay, they like my work, and I get to go to
screenings. There's the whole studio culture that I like being
in." They reached their towels and carefully sat down in the
middle of them. "I think some of Barbara's anhedonia rubs
off on me and I just start complaining to have something to
complain about."

Christopher smiled to himself. "Here's your burger."

"Yum!" Don exclaimed. "I'm so hungry I could eat a Tijuana
all-meat burrito." This was in reference to one of their running
jokes that there are no stray dogs in Tijuana.

"No, I don't think you're that hungry," Christopher amiably
disagreed.

"Yefs ow am," Don muffled through a mouthful of sourdough bun and hamburger.

Christopher stuck his tongue out with a wad of half-chewed
food on it.

Don swallowed with a disgusted frown on his face and said,
"You degenerate pig."

Christopher sneered menacingly at him, then snorted, and they both laughed. Within a few minutes, they had consumed their hamburgers and chips and had sipped down most of their lemonades. They leaned back in their beach chairs and stared out over the ocean. Don lit up a cigarette, inhaling a deep puff to the bottom of his lungs, then blew it out slowly, a smoker's sigh. Christopher bummed a cigarette from him, starting it off with a similar lazy, drawn-out sigh. Their bodies felt full and relaxed.

They watched the sunlight reflecting off the ocean in a broad, uniform glare. Their faces stung a little bit with incipient sunburn. A group of lean, muscled guys played football at the shore, sometimes sending a receiver out in the water to catch a pass. There were girls in their tight skin and colored suits, hair stringy and curled, playing Frisbee or lacrosse. Christopher squinted to see their faces, their eyes, cheeks and lips. He decided one was pretty enough; he'd take her and Don could have the rest. She had loosely curled auburn hair and a relaxed, amiable smile. She was lanky, but athletic and graceful. She looked lighthearted and alive. She reminded him of a darker version of Anne, or perhaps his sister, Elizabeth. He watched her for about half an hour, then she and her group of friends disappeared beyond the lifeguard station, leaving Christopher with a sort of philosophical sadness, openhearted and wistful, naïvely wishing they could have met, but glad they had not. He preferred to keep the romantic illusion and not muck it up with reality. Don had once defined the beach as "sun, waves and vicarious sex in more or less equal proportions," so he felt like he was meeting his "vicarious" quota.

He rolled over toward Don, feeling a sudden desire to talk for a while.

"Anne asked about you the other day."

"Oh yeah? What did she say?"

"She just asked how you were doing." Don was wearing his sunglasses and Christopher looked at his reflection in them.

"I told her you liked being at the studio, but missed messing around with the gang."

"That's true." Don started running a twig through the sand, tracing geometrical patterns of swirls and ridges.

"I told her you even said something about coming back and she said she hoped you didn't." Don raised an eyebrow. "Oh, she didn't mean it like that. She just thinks it would be a mistake. You know how much she hates it there."

"Yeah, well, none of you belong there. You're just wasting your time. You're too bright and too creative and it just sucks up your energy, then you don't have any left over to do the stuff you're supposedly using the job to support."

A group of seagulls circled above them, then swooped down to land among a pile of rocks near the shore.

"Yeah, maybe." He also began tracing patterns in the sand with a twig. "Anne said the same thing. She got real pissed off at me and Larry."

"What for?"

"Oh, I don't remember—something about getting in trouble for fooling around—making a bad enough situation worse, more draining than it already is. She gets going on one of her harangues and I just tune out." He turned his head to watch the seagulls fighting over scraps of food and garbage. Their high-pitched *screes* and *squawks* counterpointed the persistent roar of the waves, the two noises intertwining like the upper and lower voices of a fugue. Christopher continued absentmindedly, "It was something about the strain of being on Elaine's shit list making it harder for her to write at night—do you see those seagulls fighting over those potato chips?"

Don raised his head, focusing first on the birds, then on Christopher's hands in the sand. "Yeah . . . I think she's probably right."

"Well, I don't think so. I started to tell her the other day, but decided I didn't feel like arguing about it."

"She's pretty sensitive, you know, and these things upset her a lot, so I think she's got a point."

"No, she hasn't got a point at all. She's just looking for an excuse. She uses the job as an excuse, I use the job as an excuse. We're just using the fact that we have to work to survive to explain why we don't write or paint or whatever." He threw away the twig he'd been digging with. "If she wants to be a goddamn writer she should just write and quit complaining. It's just an excuse to avoid facing our weaknesses as quasi-creative people—you can't really say artists—the weaknesses in our work, the weaknesses in our self-discipline . . . If we weren't working, we'd just find other reasons to avoid facing the fact that we're scared to devote ourselves to our creative work or scared to admit we're just normal, educated bourgeoisie. So, we deceive ourselves with the notion that we may look like mild-mannered nine-to-fivers, but actually we're frustrated artists. Either way we're just looking for excuses for our failures to achieve—the great underachievers . . ."

"Yeah, well, you've gotta admit that you guys have pretty mindless jobs," Don interjected.

"It has absolutely *nothing* to do with the mindless work or even the stress. It's what we're doing there to begin with, why we got ourselves in the position of having dumb, boring jobs. I don't know who she thinks she's fooling, but it sure ain't me. If she doesn't like it, she should just quit. I'm tired of hearing all this bullshit about how bad our jobs are. It has nothing to do with the jobs. It's our chickenshitted—"

"Hold on there, boy," Don said with an amused look, "you're starting to foam at the mouth."

Christopher relaxed and a smile eased across his face. "Well, she pisses me off," he said plaintively.

"Sounds like it."

"And that's 'cause she's always complaining about how awful the job is and I never say anything. Last time I said something in the middle of one of her temper tantrums, she kicked the door—remember when she was limping around for a couple of weeks?" Don nodded. "She kicked the door to my office. Larry and I had to drag her to the hospital. She made us promise not to tell anyone how it happened. She about broke her foot and I don't even remember what it was I said. So now you know. She'd kill me if she knew I told you."

"Really? I always wondered about that broken high-heel story. Christ, there are more secrets and promises not to tell in our little clique." He seemed a little defensive from not having been included within the circle of the informed. "It doesn't make any sense 'cause we're all going to find out eventually anyway."

"Yeah, but it's another little game within the game to burn off excess energy. That's the whole thing—we have something like an extra dimension, perhaps a subliminal, primordial recollection of consciousness that gives us more imagination than we have an outlet for, so we burn it off on each other. We can tap in on it, but we can't really do anything constructive with it. It's probably all those mind-altering drugs we took. At any rate, there's not enough romance or intrigue in the system, so we manufacture it. I think that's why we turn to art: as a sort of solution. We're not artists, really. It's just someplace else to burn off excess imagination, excess energy."

"Sounds like a kind of masturbation to me."

"You've been hanging around Larry too much—he's starting to rub off on you."

"Yeah, you're right," Don said looking down, pretending to be ashamed. "I can't help it."

"Have you noticed he's been acting kind of funny lately?"

"Uh, maybe. Whaddya mean?"

"Oh, sorta stand-offish, preoccupied." Christopher squinted as if trying to focus his words. "It's like he's there, but not participating."

Don gave him a puzzled look.

"I mean, you talk to him or around him, but he's not volunteering anything. He doesn't hang out in the office and shoot the breeze anymore. There's something funny with him, but I can't put my finger on it."

"Well, he's always been big on quips and short on dialogue."

"Uh-huh."

Christopher's attention wandered to the flock of seagulls, which were taking off in a wing-flapping flurry. The rusted brown rocks looked slick and leathery, full of deep shadows, somehow lonely and deserted though surrounded by people. One last gull rose up from behind one of the boulders and flew out toward the sun. From Christopher's perspective, the stream of beach noises and sights were peculiarly arrested, as if he were looking through some psychic tunnel, watching a rock transform into a bird—a private miracle, an optical illusion whose explanation he chose to ignore a few moments for the sense of magic, then analytically accepted as the bird disappeared.

"It could be this whole thing with Anne, " Don said, continuing their conversation.

Christopher felt the clicking of a tumbler falling into place, the last piece of a combination resolving a subliminal effort to understand, the implacable door swinging open to the blinding light, an accidental pinball falling into the right hole setting off an entire Rube Goldberg contraption of intermeshing noises, events, kerplunks and lights, setting off an avalanche of psychological jackpot, as if a surreal hand materialized out of blackness above a table to provide the missing pieces of an enigmatic jigsaw puzzle. *Elementary, my dear Watson.* The whole dizzying fantasy flashed into the blue-white realization that Larry and Anne had been secretly having an affair right beneath his nose, playing him for the sucker, not letting him know the whole time. *How could I be so stupid?* he thought. *Why didn't they want me to know? Maybe we haven't been as good friends as I thought.* The structure of knowns and assumptions, the bedrock of emotional premises, began dissolving beneath him as the sinking sensation of having cockily played the fool for so many weeks roared through his mind, leaving him stunned and hurt. All the flirtation, lascivious innuendoes and teasing had not just been words. Somewhere along the line the words became flesh and he had been oblivious to it.

Christopher's mind was flooded with these thoughts, his face controlled, and as he swam through the suspicions and memories, he saw the image of Anne's sparkling freshness, that little glow on her skin, Larry's vacant desk at the office, the sort of distant, closed-off look in his eyes once when Christopher was probing why he was acting strange. Anne and Larry bursting in the door after he wrote that note. *No wonder they reacted so much. He was probably in her office with his hand up her blouse. They thought I'd found out. Sneaky sons of bitches.*

He became calculatingly aware that he was in the sensitive position of wanting to pump Don for more information without tipping Don off that he didn't know. He stared out at the horizon for several minutes, not saying anything. A cool breeze began blowing in off the ocean, signaling the waning of the afternoon. Don sat up and looked out over the water. The shadows of the guard tower and the people running along the beach were lengthening.

After a few seconds of assessing the shadows and the breeze, Don said, "I think it's about time to split."

Christopher looked up at the sun and nodded his head in agreement. "Yeah, it's beginning to cool off." He began slowly brushing sand off his legs and feet. "What do you think about this thing with Larry and Anne?" he asked as casually as possible.

Don also started brushing off sand. "Oh, I don't know." He stood up and stretched. "I know Larry's happy—well, happy isn't the word for it—he's absolutely ecstatic. I haven't talked to Anne, but from what Larry says, they seem to be fulfilling some portion of each other's dreams, which sounds fine to me. I sorta like the idea. It's only been a few weeks since they've been seeing each other in the Biblical sense, so who knows where it'll go from there." He picked up his towel and started shaking the sand off of it. "Whadda *you* think?"

Christopher remained seated on his towel, squinting at the sand. "I don't know anything about it."

Don stopped shaking his towel and looked down at Christopher. "Whaddya mean?"

"I mean I don't know anything about it."

"You mean nothing?"

"I mean I don't know anything about it."

"You mean they haven't told you yet?"

Christopher looked up at Don sheepishly. "Huh-uh."

"You're kidding," Don protested.

Christopher shook his head.

"But you work in the same office with them—how could you not know?" He collapsed back into the sand, shaking his head in disbelief. "Well, I did it again. Those two shits. I wonder why they didn't tell you. I mean, g'yod, Larry told me to keep a lid on it, but I didn't know it meant, well I assumed that, you know, you knew."

"Yeah, well, that'll teach you to assume."

"Uh-huh." Don stared at the sand between his feet. "You mean you didn't notice anything?"

"Nuh-uh," Christopher answered. "Well, now that I think about it, I know Larry wanted to jump her—we've both had this running flirtation going with her. I knew he liked her, but the last I heard, she wouldn't have anything to do with him seriously cause he was too much of an adolescent smart aleck. She told me . . . well, I guess it doesn't matter. I'm just pissed that they've gone out of their way to make sure I didn't know about it."

"Yeah, I know what you mean. Do you think it might be 'cause you're a little jealous?"

"No . . . well, maybe a little. Mostly I feel tricked and pissed."

Christopher stood up and shook out his towel. Don folded up his beach chair and piled his towel, sunglasses and sandals on top of it.

"I'm shocked, you know, like I feel like I've just had the wind knocked out of me, like this whole witty, flirtatious aspect of life has been a sham—the camaraderie, the surrogate family I'd been using to fend off work. All there is, is the job and a couple of people I work with and—stop me before I make a complete ass of myself."

"No that's OK, don't worry about it. What else?"

"Oh that's all. I don't feel like talking about it anymore. Let's get out of here."

"OK."

Christopher picked up his beach chair and towel. Don rose to follow him. The sun was still well above the horizon, a couple of hours from setting. Don said he had a couple of steaks he wanted to charbroil. They walked off toward the parking lot, Don fantasizing about the steaks, potatoes, salads and beers they were going to consume, Christopher muttering 'uh-huh' or 'yeah' as he watched his feet shuffling through the sand. Their backs and shoulders were bronzed and red, their hair matted, curling asymmetrically and lopsided off their heads. Christopher looked up at the high-rises looming above the cliffs and smiled crookedly, then turned to get one last glimpse of the sun and the beach. Breathing deep, he thought, *Another fun-filled, sunny day at the beach . . . Isn't life a dream?*

4

CHRISTOPHER HAD BEEN WORKING SINCE a little before nine. He had wandered between being depressed and being angry the rest of the weekend and was now somewhere in the middle, proofreading reports with a silent vengeance, waiting for Larry to come in so he could give the deceptive son of a bitch the cold shoulder all day.

It was a more or less typical late spring morning in L.A., gray and damp with the low clouds that crept in off the ocean during the night. Christopher had the curtains open and the dismal fogginess was pressing against the floor-to-ceiling windows. There was not much of a view; both the hills and the city were obscured. He did not care. He sat at his paper glutted desk blue-penciling the uncollated report pages, occasionally stopping to cut and paste in a letter or number.

Around ten, Dale walked in with her scheduling book. She was wearing a tentlike purple polyester top that attempted to disguise her chunky lack of a waist. Christopher glanced up, expecting Larry, and forced a smile when he saw it was Dale.

"Hi!" she said cheerfully. "How was your weekend?"

"Fine," Christopher said without any feeling. "Don and I went to the beach."

"Oh, that's nice." Dale opened the scheduling book. "Larry's not going to be up here most of the day. He's going to be in a meeting with Elaine and company, going over what has to happen before he can become an account executive. So, we're going to have to redo the schedule a little bit—you and Anne are going to have to divide up the projects he has due out today."

"Oh, great," Christopher said.

"It won't be so bad. All I'll need from you is your two Clairols and his Toyota project final-checked. Do you think you can do that?"

"Yeah," he said sullenly. It was not that much, but having to do any of Larry's work angered him. Dale walked over to Larry's desk and leafed through the disorganized pile of papers strewn over it.

"Well, it looks like it's all here and ready to go. OK?" she asked. Christopher nodded. "Good. I'll see you later." She left without further discussion.

Before he could get started on the project he'd inherited from Larry, Anne popped in the door and shut it behind her.

"Hi, sweetheart!" she said affectionately. She was wearing a silky, dark brown dress, padded at the shoulders, low cut and buttoned down the front. Her hair was pulled back straight and gathered into a sparkling net suspended behind her neck. She looked pretty and stylishly sexy. This was the way she dressed when she felt good—smooth and slim, with a hint of sin, subtly rouged cheeks, black lashes and brown eye shadow, glossy reddish-brown lipstick, nails polished to match. Her dress was gathered neatly at her waist, clinging to her bust and hips and swaying loose around her knees. Christopher took it all in in a glance and forgot he was supposed to be upset with her. Anne promptly sat down at Larry's desk and said, "I thought you might be getting lonely in here without Larry, so I decided to come give you some company."

"That was swell of ya, kid," Christopher said toughly out of the side of his mouth.

She jumped up from behind Larry's desk, pulled her dress up above her knees and swiveled so Christopher could see the backs of her legs. She was wearing seamed nylons. "What do you think?" she asked coyly.

"Yum," Christopher answered. He started clearing papers off his desk. "Here, let me make a little room for us."

Anne laughed and sat back down at Larry's desk. "Business before pleasure, honey. I was actually just coming to pick up Larry's project I'm supposed to do today and then I figured I may as well do it in here since you'll be all by your little lonesome today. Ain't I a good girl?"

"You have your moments," Christopher said without looking at her. He was beginning to remember he was mad at her and suddenly did not feel like talking to her anymore. He started putting the report pages back in place on his desk as if he were ready to get back to work.

Anne ignored his hint. She was full of talk and energy and

did not feel like working yet. She switched a lamp on over Larry's desk and leaned her elbows out on the papers in front of her so she could prop her chin in both palms. Alert and attentive, the lamplight haloing around her, she looked like a portable island of sunshine. "Whadja do this weekend?" she asked.

Christopher smirked and rolled his eyes without looking up. He knew what he was in for—she was in one of her irrepressible, invulnerably happy moods, the top end of her roller coaster, an infectious lightheartedness he ordinarily enjoyed immensely. It was now going to take a supreme effort of will to keep himself from enjoying it without letting her know he was mad at her. He was not done sulking yet. He took a deep breath and said, "Nothing much. Went to the beach, ate steaks, painted. That's all." He picked up a page and pretended to proofread it.

"Oh," Anne pouted sympathetically. "Does Chrissie have the spud boy blues?"

He smirked again without looking up. "No. I just want to get this work done—remember, editing, our jobs? What they're paying us to do here? The lecture you gave us on Friday? I'm being a good boy and getting ahead of schedule."

"Oh. OK. " Anne continued with her sympathetic coo, "Does that mean you want me to start working too?"

"Uh-huh."

"OK, I will, " she said obsequiously and began looking over the report under her elbows.

The next several minutes passed very slowly for Christopher. He made a diligent effort to pretend he was concentrating, but he had been staring at the same section of the same page for well over five minutes. He felt like every move was being monitored by Anne, who at any second, was going to figure out something was going on and start pumping him until he 'fessed up.

But she didn't. Christopher glanced over at her. She had lit up a cigarette and was studying the pages in front of her. He relaxed and noticed that he had forgotten to turn his radio on. He reached up and switched it on. Anne asked him to turn it up so she could hear it. He did. He spent a few minutes staring out the window, then began actually proofreading the page he had been staring at. They both slid into the silent rhythm of editing, alternately marking lines, cutting and pasting numbers, rereading the specification sheets, reading the audience definitions, writing in page numbers and so on. Christopher left to time a commercial script. When he returned, Anne was smoking another cigarette, still engrossed with her project. The morning was passing quickly.

By noon, they had each finished their respective projects. The sun had burned off most of the gray fog and it was beginning to look like sunny Southern California again. Christopher's resentful mood was also beginning to lighten up. Anne glanced at her watch, then looked over to Christopher, who was busily rewriting an audience definition.

"Whatcha doin' for lunch?" she asked.

"Is it lunchtime already?"

"Almost."

"Hmph. I dunno. Maybe Top Taco. What about—"

The phone started ringing on Larry's desk before he could finish. Anne picked it up.

"Hello. Anne-the-editor speaking . . . Oh, hi Minnie, what's up? . . . Oh, really?! For me? . . . I'll be right there!" She slapped the phone into place. "There's a package for me at reception!" she told Christopher. "I wonder what it is. Oh boy! I love surprises." She jumped up and ran out the door, leaving a sort of excited vacuum behind her, a lingering pocket of electrically charged air.

Christopher stared at the air. He had seen Anne get this giddy and carried away before, but only when she was drunk. This was above and beyond an infectious lightheartedness—she was dingy. He shook his head and wondered what the package was. He suddenly felt like having a smoke, so he went over to Larry's desk to see if Anne had left her cigarettes there. She had. Marlboro Lights. He tapped one out of the pack and lit it with her lighter. It tasted a little bit like tobacco. He sat back down and wondered why people smoked these lightweight cigarettes. He figured if someone were going to smoke, they might as well just do it and not fool around with these pretend cigarettes. They reminded him of the candy cigarettes he used to get when he was a kid.

Someone fumbled with the doorknob, then got it. The door swung open slowly and a vase full of flowers, not quite as large as the doorway, walked in the office. Anne was somewhere behind them and somehow managed to set them down on Larry's desk.

"Wow, that's some bouquet of flowers," Christopher remarked.

She sat down, happy and embarrassed.

"Aren't they beautiful?" she asked breathlessly. Christopher nodded. "I felt like such a jerk bringing them up the elevator, but I couldn't leave them downstairs, could I?"

Christopher was studying her very closely, watching her eyes avoiding his eyes, watching her overdo being entranced by the flowers. They were lavishly pretty flowers—about three dozen blood-red roses; uncountable sprigs of white baby's breath; red, orange, yellow and pink poppies; some sticks of purple Indian's paintbrush; and a couple of other flowers whose names Christopher did not know, all expertly arranged—an impressive vase of flowers. Christopher figured she was getting ready to lie to him about who sent them, and was attentively waiting. She was really too shocked and vulnerable to do a good job of it, and he knew he was going to catch her. The silence stretched between them like the swollen wall of an artery about to burst. Christopher looked at her expectantly as if she owed him an explanation.

"They're from my fath—" she broke off then muttered, "—er."

Christopher was staring right through her, his upper lip curled disparagingly. A layer of nervous tension, like a plastic skin, the effort of pretense, of weeks of deception, dissolved from her face. Relieved, she looked directly at Christopher, a sort of warm, pervading look. The jig was up. She smiled sheepishly and sighed, "Oh, who am I trying to fool—you know already, don't you?"

Christopher nodded, "Hm-hmm."

"How'd you find out?"

"I get around."

She folded her hands on the desk and looked down at them a few seconds, then said, "Wel-ll . . ." She wrinkled her face apologetically. "You're probably wondering why we didn't tell you." She glanced up to see Christopher nod. "Uh—m. Well, it happened sort of unexpectedly, you see, and it was sort of fun sneaking around, being the only two in on it, that sort of private world, you know. And uh . . . ," she pressed her thumbs together, "we didn't want—well, it was something we needed to work out just between the two of us . . . and it was nobody else's goddamn business."

"Uh huh," Christopher acknowledged.

"And uh-h . . . we sort of thought, well, I sort of thought that, you know, well," she took a deep breath, "that maybe someday you and I would . . . and I thought that you thought that you and I might someday . . . and so I thought you might be hurt or upset or something . . . if."

Christopher smiled. "That was a lot of thinking."

Anne smiled weakly. "Well . . . it wasn't a well-thought-out thing—I mean, we didn't sit around and plan it. It just sort of happened that way, and once it started, you know, keeping it secret and all, it just sort of continued, inertia—a secret at rest tends to stay a secret unless acted upon . . . well, anyways, we decided to just keep it that way till we saw whether it was going anywhere or was just another jump in the sack."

She looked up, grinning. "And besides, you're such a smartass, you probably would have been teasing us all the time." She looked back down at her hands. "And I didn't feel like being teased."

"So it wasn't just another jump in the sack?" Christopher asked.

"Um—," Anne shook her head, "un-huh."

"Un-huh?" Things were shifting in Christopher's mind. It felt like an amorphous mass was twisting, painlessly, into another position in his skull. "Are you in love?" he asked abruptly.

"I think so . . . maybe. He asked me to marry him."

Christopher coughed. "He what?!!"

"Saturday night, he . . . uh . . . asked me to, you know, marry him."

"Are you kidding me?" Christopher's self-assured composure began slipping away. "And what did you say?"

"Oh, nothing . . . yet." She pulled one of the roses out of the vase. "He's trying to formulate a sentimental basis for a positive shift in attitude."

Christopher was stunned. Not in his wildest, most extrapolative imagination had it occurred to him that their affair, that Larry's intention, was any more than a lust-sparked, desire-driven fling. Larry was too flippant, too flirtatious, too hedonistic. But he was also too honest, usually painfully, bluntly honest, to ask Anne to marry him unless he really meant it.

"Is it . . . working?"

"Yeah, I think so." She sniffed the rose. "No one has ever sent me flowers like this before. For such a cynical smart aleck, he's very romantic. And I'm not getting any younger."

"Hmph," Christopher snorted.

"What do you mean, 'Hmph'?" she asked defensively.

"I mean twenty-four, or is it twenty-five, is hardly old enough to start diving into a marriage for fear of becoming an old maid."

"So you don't think we should get married?" She seemed hurt and disappointed. Christopher noticed the sensitive disappointment and was acutely aware of the fragile vulnerability, of how much Larry had evidently touched her.

"Un-huh. I'm not saying that," he said quickly. "It was just a humph about you're not getting any younger."

"Well, then, what do you think?"

Christopher took a deep breath and let it out slowly. "I think . . . you'd better give me a cigarette."

Anne tossed him a cigarette and her lighter. He lit it slowly and took a couple of long, reflective drags. Things were shifting fast and he needed a few minutes to get his thoughts sorted out. He stared out the window, gazing at the grizzled hills. His mind scanned through the last few weeks—Anne's radiance and love-struck giddiness; Larry's peculiar diffidence, probably shyness, such an unusual quality for someone like him; Larry's rapt gaze as Anne lectured them on Friday; the multitude of glances and touches he had taken for flirtatious jokes.

"I think—," he paused dramatically, casually tapping his cigarette ash onto his desk, staring into the middle of the office.

"You think what?" Anne asked impatiently, knowing he was stretching it out just to tease her.

"I think . . . I think you'd be a fool to give up a chance like this."

"You do?"

"Christ yeah," he asserted. "Larry's bright, quick-witted, fun-loving, healthy and energetic, has good teeth—," Anne smiled at his horse joke, "tall, dark, and handsome, though a little on the hairy side—"

"He is not!" Anne said, mocking indignance and laughing.

"For an Episcopalian Jew you couldn't get a better deal." Anne broke out laughing. Christopher took another drag off his cigarette. "And besides, for someone like Larry to be willing to commit himself to the point of asking you to marry him, I don't think he's fooling around or being flippant—he must really mean it. I think he's genuinely in love with you. Something about you has opened up that place in him where he can be romantic and idealistic, even sentimental and sensitive. And he's obviously done the same thing with you—I've never seen anyone as dingy and radiant as you've been lately. There's something different about you—like an extra layer of prettiness—I figured it was just cause you were getting laid." Anne grabbed a grammar book and threw it at him. Christopher effortlessly dodged it and continued as if nothing had occurred. "No, honestly, I've noticed something different about you lately, something good . . . and I think it's directly linked to Larry. I don't think you have any choice—I think you're fated to be mated."

Christopher knew he was exaggerating a bit, but he liked the way the rhyme rolled off his tongue. It was true enough, though. Larry was a good match for her, and he, for one, never would have married Anne. Her volatile, unpredictable moods would have driven him crazy. A few jumps in the sack, maybe a convenient urban relationship, but not marriage. Larry was willing to go the whole route, so the best thing, the most Bogartian thing to do, was pave the way without interfering.

"You don't think he's just adolescently smitten?" Anne asked.

"Unh-uh."

"You don't think I'm too neurotic for him?"

"Unh-uh."

"You wanna go to Top Taco?"

Christopher smiled. "Sure."

Anne jumped up and held out her arm for Christopher to escort her. They smiled conspiratorially and left for Top Taco.

They took a relatively long lunch. Top Taco was an Armenian-owned fast food Mexican joint near the corner of Sunset and La Brea. It had an open-air patio which was good for conversational lunches. Christopher was hooked on their combination burritos and saw to it he got a Top Taco fix at least once or twice a week. Anne did not particularly care for Mexican food, so she did most of the talking and Christopher listened. She gave him a detailed account of the genesis of the romance, when it started, how she would not have anything to do with Larry and why, how he disabused her of her prejudices, how he helped her through a couple of severe depressions, where they went on their first dates, how charming and sensitive he was outside of work, the first night they slept together, how he seduced her or rather how they seduced each other, what a passionate and considerate lover he was, the antics they went through to keep it a secret, times they almost got caught, the time Larry's little sister did catch them having sex in his roommate's hot tub when Larry's parents were visiting. She also told Christopher that she had come to work in his office that morning planning to tell him all about it because she needed someone to talk to, but when she saw what a bad mood he was in, she had changed her mind. That made sense to Christopher; he thought it had been a little too easy to get her to confess.

By the time they returned to the office, Anne was much less giddy and seemed more like her old self. Talking to Christopher had relieved the need for outbursts of dinginess. The pressure of suppressing all that feeling had exaggerated its intensity beyond her control, but now she was back to a smooth-flowing simmer. She still glowed or radiated a sort of deep contentment, but it no longer had the aura of glee with it. Christopher was relaxed and lighthearted, happy to have resolved the tension between them, happy to be her confidante. Neither of them felt like working. Anne twirled one of her roses in her fingers, careful not to get poked by a thorn. Christopher was slumped down in his chair, resting his head on the chair's back.

"What's going to happen when Anne the writer becomes Mrs. Larry?" Christopher asked after a while.

Anne twirled the rose a few times. "Oh, I dunno. I . . . I think I've just been kidding myself. I'm not, and probably never will be, a serious contender for any literary accolades. Art for art's sake doesn't fill any refrigerators. I'll probably commit the modern sin of becoming a moderately happy housewife . . . who has the pages of two or three unfinished manuscripts strewn around the guest bedroom floor, provided, of course, we ever own a house."

"Sounds like you're throwing in the towel."

"Yeah. Sorta. I don't want to sound like I'm jumping on the opportunity to get married just to avoid the exigencies of writing. I just feel . . . I just feel like it's not worth it anymore. And anyways, I wouldn't be a housewife exactly. I'll still have to work." She raised the rose up to her nose and sniffed it. She continued breathing through it as she spoke. "I can't take this anymore." She flicked the rose towards Larry's desk, indicating the report pages. "I mean I can't take this being in between nine-to-fiving and writing. My parents have been waiting for me to get it out of my system and grow up and do something that's for real, like making babies." She smiled crookedly. "Well, this should make them real happy. Did you ever wonder why you keep on painting?"

"Oh," Christopher drawled, "not more than five or ten times a day."

"Right!" she laughed, "me too. Well, why do you keep doing it?"

Christopher shrugged. "I keep getting ideas. I mean a day hardly goes by without my getting another idea for something."

"Yeah, but why?" Anne persisted.

"I dunno exactly. Like the other day, I was sitting here looking out the window, looking at the hills." He turned his head to stare at the hills again. He paused a few seconds as he recalled the idea. "And I was just sitting here, and the hills suddenly looked like the buried spines and ribs of giant dinosaurs or iguanas. You know what I mean? And then I got this idea of the sky clumping up and changing color, fast, and the hills started moving and two big iguana-like beasts shook the dirt and trees off their backs and started fighting, spilling their guts down Laurel Canyon." He stopped a second. "That's all wordy and prosaic and doesn't capture it at all—there was this special . . . penetrating feeling to it and I wanted to get it down somehow, express it. So, I went home and laid out some sketches for a series of paintings. I see them as a series of more or less Oriental landscapes, with that detail and mistiness, but the sky and the dragons or dinosaurs would be layered, glazed enamel paint, almost ceramic and metallic, the paint so thick that they're in slight relief, not just two-dimensional. The whole thing would be connected like one of those paneled room dividers—you know what I mean?" She nodded. "Now who the hell knows what it's all about, why, where it comes from, who'll want to buy a picture of a dinosaur fight? It doesn't make any sense, but what am I supposed to do with these ideas?"

"Sounds like you'd have done the world a favor by suppressing that one," Anne said sarcastically. "You have a fucking weird imagination. Maybe you missed your calling at Marvel Comics."

"Quit being so goddamned literal," Christopher chided.

"But that's just my point. I've been thinking a lot about this lately, especially this weekend. This thing with the dinosaurs, it's sort of hokey, but it must have meant something to you or it wouldn't have had enough impact to make you think twice about it. And maybe it's a metaphor for the wells of raw energy deep in our psyches, buried by layers of civilization's silt, but still forming the structural foundation for what we see today, that maybe there's a way of tapping or releasing that energy. OK, so I buy the idea, maybe even like it, but who cares? It's still just a goddamn canvas with paint on it and we're still here, having to pay the rent next Monday. It all seems so insipidly futile, and yet you keep on doing it. There's really no market— well, almost no market—for this type of stuff, it's idiosyncratic symbolism—so where does that leave you? Painting lingerie ads? That wouldn't do the trick. It's not just painting that does the trick. It's expressing ineffable ideas and emotions—cleverly, craftily, beautifully doing something that approximates a vision. Right?" Christopher nodded. "You can't support yourself with it, you aren't independently wealthy, so you end up working at a place like this, neither an artist nor a dedicated worker, in limbo. And this isn't enough. I didn't like being a poor writer and I don't like being a cog in someone's assembly line. I can't commit myself to either one—did you ever read Dante's *Divine Comedy*?"

"No." Christopher smiled. "We were supposed to read part of it in high school, but I just read the *Cliff Notes*."

"Well, it doesn't matter. There's a section of purgatory where he describes an antechamber filled with angels who were not rebels, they didn't side with Lucifer in his rebellion, but they weren't faithful or loyal to God, either. They were uncommitted. Dante scorns the people and the angels in this antechamber and says they never were really alive—to have real life demands a kind of commitment, and lacking that, you end up like us, in limbo. I've always remembered that section—I reread it every once in a while. I thought once that I could commit myself to writing, to the life of the artist, that would be my redemption, my salvation: my highest priority would be my creativity. That's a tough life and I'm not that tough." She waited for Christopher to say something. He said nothing, so she continued.

"I've been extremely happy with Larry the last several weeks—it's had its ups and downs, but all in all, I've never felt so full of hope and life and I haven't written a thing, you see . . . I haven't written a thing." She paused a few seconds and set the rose down on the desk with an unnecessary carefulness. "I'm not going to give it up completely, you know. I mean, I'll still have the urge, I'll still have the dream. I just won't be the next Virginia Woolf or a female incarnation of Salinger. I never would have been—I don't have the drive—and there's no sense making the rest of my life miserable trying. I'll do what I can commit myself to with all my heart . . . and sometimes I'll write. It's just a change in priorities. A marriage, a family, and a few short stories and poems are enough to keep me occupied for the next twenty or thirty years. I think I have a chance at being happy at something and I think I'm going to take it."

"Well, sweetheart, it's your life and I can't say I haven't thought of the same thing myself. I think marrying Larry is a good idea, but I don't see the need to drop your dreams for the sake of getting married. It's not a particularly safe investment these days."

"I'm not dropping them."

"OK. Well, at any rate, you've got that sixth sense, a sort of extrasensory perception, like a seedling growing under asphalt that will find an outlet despite any obstacles, popping up in the weirdest places."

"I know that," Anne said with slight edge of impatience.

"I think you can do both."

"I will. I just won't be measuring the success or failure of a day by how much I write—it will be another dimension, but not the only dimension of my life. You see what I mean?"

"Yeah, I guess so," Christopher conceded, smiling.

The conversation dropped off into a pensive silence. After a few minutes, Anne pushed herself away from Larry's desk.

"Well," she said, "I think I'd better get back to work." She stood up to leave. "I think I'm going to be giving notice soon." The smile melted from Christopher's face. "Larry's downstairs telling them he's planning to move back to New York in two months, with the company or without, so I'll probably quit before that and start getting things ready to go."

Christopher's heart began thumping hard. In the back of his mind he'd known that eventually they would be leaving, but the thought of not having them there to tease, to banter with, to breathe and talk with, had not really emerged. He saw their life together in and around the office like a soap bubble growing frail, glassy and transparent, moving through one last rotation, then bursting. It suddenly made him very sad. He tried to suppress it before Anne noticed. He glanced down at her legs. "Hey, mamacita," he said as if he had not heard her. He had a lecherous grin on his face. "Are those real seamed nylons or Sears seamed nylons?"

She walked over to him, swiveled, and pulled her dress up as if she had to check and see. "Real ones, you syphilitic progeny of a demented mud slug—Christ have you got a unidimensional mind," she jeered affectionately. "Now admit it, worm brain, you're gonna miss me."

"I admit nothing to degenerate, phlegm-sodden spinach brains like you."

Anne bent over and kissed him on the lips. "That's OK," she whispered, "I know."

She jumped up and waved goodbye by wiggling her painted nails over her shoulder as she walked out the door.

A lonely silence slowly filled the room while Christopher systematically glanced from place to place as if trying to imprint the room indelibly in his memory. He gazed at Larry's sloppy desk and smiled when he saw Larry's spare X-acto knife sticking out of the wall. Everything seemed to become conspicuously rectangular and hard-edged. He looked at the rectangular shape of their desks, the rectangular shape of the report folders, grammar books, and specifications sheets. His radio. The office itself. The windows. The walls covered with muddy-yellow business wallpaper, the worn carpet covering the floor. The room was filled with market research reports, file folders and correction tape. That was the way it would be after they left—just another office, no longer a refuge. He felt like a round peg hiding out in a square hole, and he wanted out. He hoped Elaine would do him a favor and fire him. He could probably get a couple of good months' painting done on his severance and vacation pay, maybe more if he budgeted it out with his savings.

Christopher's gaze wandered out his window. It went past Dar Magreb's parking lot and over the purple-bloomed trees, to the terraced homes clinging to the hillsides. His eyes settled on the grizzled spines of the hills. They did look just like buried spines of giant dinosaurs. He smiled to himself and let the image of the beasts stirring up to fight run through his mind's eye. He watched the clouds clumping, the sky turning to that peculiar emerald green. The flash of raw energy in their eyes as they maneuvered to strike each other. The second beast suddenly jumped and ripped a long, deep gash into the first one's flesh, and it collapsed in a lifeless heap. The second one blinked and twisted its head to the side, staring at its victim.

It started to turn away, but something began stirring within the lifeless pile of flesh. The air surrounding it shimmered and became an iridescent turquoise. The gutted flesh stirred again and ripped open. Through the bloody gash burst a brilliantly colored phoenix, an immense, eagle-like bird that instantly sprang clear of the carnage. With its dark eyes burning and one thrust of its wings, it flew off into the emerald sky, leaving the second lizard blinking and twisting its head from side to side as if it were trying to figure out what happened.

"She's right," Christopher thought, "I do have a fucking weird imagination."

He picked up his X-acto knife and tossed it into his blotter a couple of times, then made a mental note to remember to do a sketch of the bird when he got home that evening.

Between Shadows

NIEN WANG entered his room quietly. It was dark, warm and full of his mementos. He slipped past ornamental swords and colorful silk tapestries of dragons and courtesans. There were jade statues, watercolors of Buddhist retreats and leatherbound books with gold-laminated Chinese titles. This was his sanctuary. He could walk through its shadowy dimness without stumbling. He knew exactly where everything was placed, and bumped into nothing.

He actually preferred having the room dark or semi-lit. It was one of his habits to enter the room and weave his way to the back, then couch himself in the satin pillows against the far wall. After working the pillows into a comfortable position, he would let his attention wander from object to silhouetted object, recalling in colorful detail their sunlit appearance. It was as if his mind and the room merged into the nether realm between imagination and fact. It was this meditative state of in-betweenness that he lived for above all other things.

The room was not stuffy, but had a light, sweet odor of cherry blossoms. It was clean, dustless and pervaded with an aura not so much of age, but of timelessness. Nien Wang himself was clean and timeless. His back was straight and his eyes were clear, though he was an old man. His face was leathery and wrinkled, his cheeks hollow, and his goatee thin and white. He had outlived his sons and daughters. His wife had died before them. He was now the ancient patriarch of his granddaughter's house, but he was only a shadow of a grandfather and rarely assumed the authority of a patriarch. He spent most of his time up in his room musing, performing T'ai Chi or reading.

This time, as usual, he crossed the room to the far wall and sat on the satin pillows, wearing his favorite smoking jacket, also made of satin. He fingered some of the intricate gold embroidery, the patterns of dragons interlaced among patterns of plum blossoms. He envisioned how it looked when his wife had given it to him fifty-five—or was it sixty—years ago. He had treated the jacket with the utmost care and it still retained much of its original beauty. He thought about his wife and the jacket for several minutes, concluding his reverie with the thought, *Oh rarely, rarely the time is given. I wish we could sport but a little longer.* This was the way he ended most of his reveries, quoting from "The Book of Odes," "The Nine Songs," or some such classical Chinese poem, attempting to encapsulate the feeling of the reverie as briefly and accurately as possible. It was a game he used to play with his friend, Pan Ku, before the latter's death.

He thought of Pan Ku's elaborate wit and smiled. He remembered the oxbone pipe Pan Ku had given him. Pan Ku claimed to be a direct descendant, perhaps even a reincarnation, of the famous Han poet of the same name. For years, Nien Wang teased him about his self-inflating memory, and they would have long arguments over the details of Pan Ku's life. Nien Wang always tried to trip up his friend by asserting falsehoods about Pan Ku's homosexuality or impotence to get Pan Ku to cite some biographical source quoting satisfied lovers and thus prove that instead of recalling the details from his past life, Pan Ku had actually read them from this book or that.

One year Pan Ku presented Nien Wang with the oxbone pipe, telling Nien that the filigreed engravings on it were the palatial estate in which he had written his poetry in the previous life. That ended the argument for Nien. The grace which emanated from Pan Ku's carvings was enough proof for him—that quality of beauty could only be inspired by a kind of truth that transcended mere factual accuracy.

Nien reached for the shadow of a small stand near the pillows.

Without fumbling, he picked up the old pipe, some matches and tobacco. "Pan Ku,"' he thought as he packed some tobacco in, "I dedicate this bowl to you, you old wine sponge." He lit a match. As the yellow spark of phosphor briefly illuminated the room, a flash of brilliant colors and sharply defined boundaries of objects leapt before him. Nien sucked the flame down inside the bowl, and through the orange glow of the tobacco, he saw the silhouette of a small boy sitting in front of him. It was his six year old great-grandson, Hsiao.

"Hsiao Tang Lang, is that you, you little imp?" Nien demanded with a feigned irritation.

"Yes, Grandfather, it's me."

Nien admired his deferential, but fearless, reply. It pleased him to know that this poised little child was part of his line. "I'm not your grandfather, I'm your great-grandfather. How many times do I have to remind you?" Hsiao said nothing. Still pretending to be irritated, Nien continued, "How long have you been in here?"

"I heard you coming up the stairs and ran in to wait for you."

Nien snorted and smiled. It disturbed him to think he had not detected his great-grandson's presence, but at the same time, he was proud of Hsiao's ability to remain so quiet. *This little nymph has great spirit,* he thought. "So what are you bothering me for, grasshopper?"

"Do you want to play checkers?" Hsiao replied. This was a code developed between them which meant he wanted Nien Wang to tell him a story.

"Oh no, Hsiao Tang. I'm much too busy to idle away my time playing checkers with a little grasshopper."

This was their code for "OK, what would you like to hear a story about?"

"I beg your pardon, Great-grandfather. Are you thinking about what happened after you burned the evil magician's pagoda down to the ground and left only smoldering ashes and powdered bones?"

Nien Wang smiled thinly and drew a long, contemplative drag from his pipe, then let it out slowly. "Ah yes, Hsiao, that's exactly what I was thinking about. Only Li Pa wasn't an evil magician, just a rival dabbler in mystical powers. You remember, of course, that Li Pa and I competed for the Ch'in Emperor's favor, whose school was the better school. We had been close friends in our youth—almost inseparable, so no, he wasn't an evil magician. He was very bitter when I did win the Emperor's favor. Yes, indeed, very bitter. Many of his companions spread malicious rumors about my having cheated, and when Li Pa's favorite son was killed near my school, the same rumormongers made him believe I had had him killed as a warning or a punishment. Li Pa was consumed with grief and he turned his mystical powers to vengeance, calling on darker forces, and this warped him terribly."

"So you burned his evil pagoda to the ground, leaving only smoldering ashes and powdered bones," Hsiao interrupted.

"Ah yes." Nien Wang smiled at Hsiao's propensity for recalling the morbid parts of the tales most clearly. "That eventually did occur—it was a terrible incident and I should never have become so enraged by his desire for vengeance against me— but I was full of pride and was insulted that he was accusing *me*, the great mystical scholar and favorite of the Emperor, of being a cheat and a murderer. I should have thought of him as the old friend of my youth, but no, I let my suspicion and anger dominate me and that brought a very tragic end to Li Pa, not a noble way of treating a former friend. That was very bad indeed."

"But what happened then, Great-grandfather?" Hsiao reminded him of his original request. Nien Wang was going through his usual pattern of summarizing the previous story, trying to inculcate its moral. Hsiao always sat patiently through this, but eventually would nudge Nien to get on with the new story. Nien accepted this prodding as a matter of course and smiled at his grandson's temerity.

"Ah yes, well, I resigned from the Emperor's service and withdrew to the country. I realized that greed for power and status had led to the death of a once-good man and good friend. Yes, I became a country farmer and died very peacefully."

"That's all?" Hsiao asked.

"Yes, I'm afraid so. You see, Li Pa was dead and so there wasn't much more that could happen, was there?"

"No sir, I guess not," Hsiao replied politely.

"After that I avoided the subject of mysticism altogether. By my next life, I'd completely forgotten all about it. I'm sure you'd be much too bored to hear about that life, wouldn't you?"

Hsiao sighed with an edge of exasperation. This was another of his great-grandfather's coded statements that meant he had a story ready to be told. To be respectful, Hsiao would have to listen to it, and pretend to enjoy it, though he really wanted to hear more about Li Pa.

Nien Wang pretended to ignore the sigh.

"Oh no, Great-grandfather, I'd be very interested in hearing about it," Hsiao answered, frowning inside and wishing he had not gotten Nien Wang rambling. Nien could talk the scales off a goldfish if he wanted to. When it was a good story, it did not matter, but Hsiao could feel a long, involved story coming on and was not sure if he could put up with the whole thing. Nien Wang leaned over to the stand near the pillows and lit a scented candle.

"Well, Hsiao, as you know, the Han dynasty was a great dynasty, the dynasty in which Confucianism was accepted as the state religion. Emperor Wu decreed it officially. And, in accordance with Confucian doctrine, civil exams were given for the preparation of statesmen. I had passed my exam and was a medium-level statesman, though I was still considered a student. I wore my plain blue coat as students always wore. After I passed the exam, I was married to a pretty girl named Shu Nu. Oh, she was very pretty indeed. She had a natural scent of delicious perfume, her brows arched delicately, her eyes radiated the glowworm's light. Oh, very beautiful. Most beautiful, yes. We had a son, a red-cheeked, smiling infant. We were a happy family. I was a diligent apprentice. I studied my Shih Ching and could advise my superior on which sections to quote to make his complaints or praises to the emperor. I worked for Yueh-fu, the music bureau, and helped collect folk poetry, as Confucius had done 100 years before with the Shih Ching. I was called Chih Ku, one whose aim is at antiquity. We led quite an idyllic life, Shu Nu and I."

Hsiao squirmed a little and tried to hide his growing discomfort. This sounded very much like a story Nien had told before. The golden glow of the candle flame flickered against a silk wall hanging of a dragon so that all its scarlets and yellows appeared to dance between the shadows.

After taking a few lazy puffs of his pipe, Nien continued his story. "On my days off, we would walk through the city, through its gardens and fish markets. There was one particular park we loved to wander through. It had a stream that shimmered in the sunlight." Nien made a trickling motion with his hands. "The stream spilled into ponds where carp, dace and sheatfish would arch their backs and twitch their tails. The waters were loud with a multitude of living things. There were moon-bright pearls gleaming on the pond slopes while quartz, chrysoberyl and clear crystal glittered, catching and throwing back a hundred colors from where they lay tumbled on the stream bottom. The banks were blanketed with green orchids and hidden beneath selenia. There were wild geese, swans, cranes and night herons that settled upon the waters, drifting lightly over the surface. This was a very special park, Hsiao, very special.

"At the end of the fifth month of the thirty-fifth year of Emperor Wu's reign, we were on one of our customary excursions. The three of us walked shy and content, our life the reward of devoted service to a good emperor. My pretty wife, with her black hair short cropped and straight, held our child against her side. They clung together like two flowers leaning cheek to cheek. In our indigo smocks, we walked the streets of the capital and quietly absorbed the warm spring."

Hsiao tried to squirm imperceptibly again. Nien Wang's mouth had the faintest hint of a smile and his eyes sparkled in the candle light.

"Where's your mother, little squirmer? Isn't it time for you to go to bed?"

"Oh no, not yet, Great-grandfather," Hsiao assured him. Anything was better than having to go to bed, and despite the monotony of the flowery story, he enjoyed just being in Nien Wang's room, in Nien Wang's presence. "She'll come get me when it's time."

"Well, in that case, I'll continue," Nien said. "Where did I leave off, Hsiao Tang?"

This was a test to make sure Hsiao listened carefully. Hsiao knew this and without hesitating said, "You and Shu Nu were in indigo smocks walking through the streets of the capital city."

"Ah yes, I remember now. We were heading for the park again. We walked along a path that had high, wood slat fences over which hung mulberry trees. The mulberries were just little green buds where blossoms had been a few weeks earlier.

"As we drifted down this path, three men appeared ahead of us. We looked up and began to smile, but faster than our most lightning-quick reflexes, they reached into their belts and hurled backhanded three long wooden darts that pierced our heads as though they were pieces of fruit. Shu Nu dropped our baby onto the ground like a bag of fish. I saw the dart sticking through Shu Nu's head and the blood trickling down her face. Before I could protest or utter a cry, we were all dead."

Hsiao's eyes had popped wide open and his mouth formed a small oval. Nien Wang's eyes smiled—he had tricked little Hsiao again.

"Oh, the anguish and sorrow we felt as our pained eyes met, the last image, the last sight. The tremendous desire to touch and embrace, to caress and say goodbye, but all being said by the last flicker in our eyes."

Nien Wang paused to puff on his pipe. Hsiao fixed his gaze on Nien Wang, anxious for him to continue.

"From a short distance we looked like three posters pinned to the wall. Too much, too much, was the pain and injustice, swirling and rushing around us. Dizzy. The three men continued coming toward us when suddenly—" Nien made a quick whooshing motion toward Hsiao, and Hsiao flinched. "The chilling, terrible growl of the sick Li Pa beast burst from within them, overwhelming and terrifying! The cold black evil lifted a veil and revealed his green and purple skin, his sunken dark eyes—pupils glowing with yellow fire, lips parched and cracked, blood and pus oozing from them. Cackling, the beast pounced upon my spirit."

"No, Grandfather, no!" Hsiao shouted and grabbed his hair.

Nien Wang lowered his voice to a dramatic whisper. "And there I was, my body dead, and my soul about to be consumed by the dreadful Li Pa beast."

Nien Wang's eyes caught the flame of the candle and for a second they looked to Hsiao as though they had the yellow fire in them. Hsiao hid his eyes and shouted "No! Don't get me, Li Pa. Help me, help!"

Nien ignored his exhortations. "I was like a bird before a snake, frozen. The horror of the beast swept over me. I tried to go into a meditative trance, but it was hopeless. All my energy was sucked away. All the while, Li Pa's cackle echoed through the horrid gloominess. My last conscious decision was just to let it all happen and not flinch; I would be like a rock letting the thundering rapids rush over me."

Hsiao uncovered his eyes. "And then what happened, Grandfather?" From downstairs, Nien Wang heard his granddaughter, Mo Hsin, calling for Hsiao. He decided to ignore her till he finished the story.

"After a long spell of acting like a rock, I opened my spirit's eyes and there sat Li Pa before me, rolling around on the ground laughing. 'Ah, the turtle has finally come out of his shell,' he said."

"Hsiao, are you up here?"

Nien and Hsiao looked at each other conspiratorially. They were hoping Mo Hsin would go back downstairs.

Hsiao whispered, "And then what, Great-grandfather?"

"The illusion of worldly life fell from my eyes and Li Pa and I embraced. He had taught me a painful lesson, a very sad lesson but a necessary one, and I was grateful. We waited many years to incarnate again."

"And what lesson was that, Great-grandfather?"

Mo Hsin stood in the doorway. She saw the two of them leaning together and whispering. She reached inside the door and flicked the light switch on. The veil of darkness vanished and the two of them lay exposed to Mo Hsin's glare. Her eyes were fuming and her bright red lips were pursed with anger.

"Hsiao, what the hell are you doing in here?" she demanded, "You're supposed to be in bed!"

"Grandfather was telling me about his former life."

"He's not your grandfather, he's your *great-grandfather*, an old man with a fixation on the past—" She glared into Nien Wang's eyes—"a past that has no place today. They're not past lives, they're figments of his hyperactive imagination, an imagination he uses to scare little boys half out of their wits!"

"No, he—" Hsiao tried to interrupt.

"I heard you screaming, so don't try to deny it. You've been having nightmares ever since the last story he told you! Now come here."

Hsiao rose reluctantly and walked over to her.

"We have a perfectly good color TV; I don't know why you can't watch it." She tugged his tee shirt over his head and pulled off his tennis shoes. "There, now go to bed. And don't forget to take your socks off."

Hsiao left and Mo Hsin stood in the doorway. Nien Wang was staring at the floor in front of him. Several seconds passed before she spoke.

"Grandpa, don't you understand?" she pleaded. "Things are different now. Hsiao loves you, but he's too impressionable—he believes everything you say is fact, but there isn't a world out there for him to go to where it is fact. I can't let him grow up in a world that doesn't exist . . . don't you see?

Nien Wang raised his eyes. There was a distant look in them. He glanced down at the oxbone pipe Pan Ku had given him, then back up at Mo Hsin. He smiled sympathetically and nodded.

"Thanks, Grandpa, thanks," Mo Hsin said sincerely. "Would you like the lights off?"

Nien nodded again. Mo Hsin switched the lights off and went back downstairs. Nien Wang sighed and refilled his pipe, thinking of Pan Ku. His fingers traced the engravings of the ancient palatial estate as he wondered what the old wine sponge was up to now.

Another Day in L. A.

or

*What to Do about the Inevitable
Nuclear Holocaust*

THE funny thing is, you know, is that I didn't even know the guy.

But first things first.

That's what he said to me, "But first things first . . ."

The air rippled above the pavement. It was the middle of the afternoon in the middle of the summer in the middle of Los Angeles. It wasn't actually Los Angeles, it was Beverly Hills. The streets were empty. For that matter, so were the sidewalks, except for the little ripples of heat. There was an echo of droning air conditioners, all in a line. The sidewalks merged into an empty "v" dwindling into the western horizon. They were white and the buildings were white, except for the green awnings that cast a slightly cooler shadow than the rest of the air. That's where I was standing—in the shade of an awning. It was not the sort of day for an old man in a tweed suit, tie and full white beard to be watching TV through a picture window. I guess that's what caught my attention. Just outside my shade, this little man stopped to watch TV. He looked up at me—I guess it was then that I noticed he did not have a full white beard. The heat was rippling up around his face. Funny thing to imagine a full white beard. But it was hot and he did have a little white moustache and long white hair.

He stepped into my shade and said, "But first things first . . ." He had watery blue eyes and gestured "first" with a stubby finger.

I think that was the way he usually introduced himself. If the person didn't turn around and run, he went on. I didn't particularly want to leave my shade, so he continued.

"Dreams are realities just like the reality you're seeing me in is a reality."

Poor little guy, the heat was getting to him.

"Their reality isn't any less valid than this reality—they're just permutations of the same basic reality generators: each individual's hopes, goals, expectations, plans, etc. These envisioned desires exist someplace. They exist here to the degree we all share them." He sweated to get that one out. I thought he was going to faint or something. Next he was going to tell me he was Tinker Bell about to disappear because all the little kiddies play video games and don't even know who Peter Pan is these days. I mean, this guy was weird.

And being the incorrigible smart aleck my mother has always accused me of being, I asked, "So am I dreaming you, or what?"

He really liked that. He about laughed his pudgy little stomach off. I put my hand on his shoulder because I thought he was going to keel over or something. Never can tell with these old folks, you know. My hand didn't sink into the twilight zone or anything, but I did notice that it wasn't actually a tweed suit he was wearing but a gray flannel one.

"No—" he said between breathless chuckles, "No—I'm doing enough dreaming for both of us."

He wrapped his arm around my shoulder. A silver Rolls Wraith slid up beside the curb. Its uniformed chauffeur jumped out and opened the rear door, then stood at chauffeur attention. The little man nudged me toward the car. I did not have anything better to do that afternoon, so I sort of just went with the flow. That's what I thought, "Go with the flow, kiddo." I was thinking in prosaic rhymes those days. Not that they were prose rhymes but—well, you know what I mean.

So anyways, there I was in the back seat of this British ocean liner, being served strawberry margaritas by a pudgy little man with stubby fingers in a gray flannel suit. The whole time he's chattering away like he was in a hurry or something.

"There are other places, you know, where there are slightly different concepts of reality that intermesh to form a different set of events. Australian aborigines, Markab, the KKK, you know. Just other permutations of reality."

My strawberry daiquiri—no, it was a margarita, wasn't it?—was outstanding. The car was air conditioned and something else, like he had oxygen pumped in or maybe one of those negative ionizers. Whatever it was, the air was different in there; it felt good. I started wondering how this lunar module heading for Uranus managed to stay so rich. "Must have good attorneys," I thought. "Probably should have gone to law school like my mom said." Moms are always right about that sort of thing.

The little man tapped me on the knee. It suddenly hit me what he was after. The little man was a little fag. I started feeling creepy and naïve and dumb all at the same time. Brother—you just can't trust anybody these days, I thought.

He tapped me on the knee again. I looked at him. He had his strawberry margarita gripped between two fingers that looked like they were too short to hold the glass that way and any minute it was going to pop out like a bar of soap and make a mess all over the nice plush interior. But it didn't. He just kept talking.

"When you're dreaming, you move into a reality that doesn't intermesh completely with this one."

I felt like that most of the time, so that was nothing new to me. I mean, I felt like I was not exactly intermeshing as we crossed Sunset into Bel-Air, if you know what I mean.

"Sometimes it's very similar and thus easily remembered."

"Pardon me, sir, but what is easily remembered?" Somewhere along there he started talking with a British accent and I thought I might be sitting next to some exiled duke or earl, which is why they let him run around the way he was. I figured I had better start acting polite, at least pretend I was listening. The guy might want a secretary or a butler or something, one never knows. I mean the guy was rich. May as well make a good impression on him, I thought.

So anyways, "Dreams," he said. "The thing to know about all this is you don't have to be fixated into a particular network of linear events, a reality. You can change realities. You're not limited to a single linear string of events. You're not linear— you're sort of translinear."

I decided he wasn't a little fag after all—he was just weird.

"Right, translinear," I said.

"You can move from permutation to permutation at will, if you get good at it."

"I guess you have to get pretty good, huh?"

"Yes, exactly. The only thing is that you carry your subconsciously envisioned dreams, plans and so forth which will, at some point, find enough agreement to intermesh and become real. Which is to say if you're permuting to avoid something, forget it. It'll always catch up with you."

We were winding around into the nether regions of places I had never been before. They were nice enough homes, when you could see them through the bushes and fences. My glass was empty and he, the little man/potential little fag/full-fledged lunar module, poured me another one. His was empty, too, so he stopped talking long enough to pour himself another. His deft movements with his stubby little hands made me smile. Then he started off again like he was in a race or something.

"Unresolved dreams always come up again and again. You keep re-experiencing them like a record player that plays the same record over and over again. You can avoid listening to a particular section you dislike by moving the playing arm back or forward, but as long as that record is there and the playback mechanism is on, that section is going to happen again and again and again."

We pulled into the driveway of a three-story, red colonial brick mansion with a large sweeping lush green lawn and gardens thrown in here and there like a flowery golf course for midget gardeners who golfed balls of flower seeds—well,

I guess I'm getting carried away. It was a nice place, and let's leave it at that.

As he was saying, "That section is going to happen again and again and again," the Rolls pulled to a stop and the chauffeur opened the door nearest the little man. "Which is what this trip is about: changing records."

I thought maybe he was going to offer me a job. Instead he hopped out of the seat and motioned for me to follow him. The chauffeur stood at implacable attention. I winked at him to see what he would do. He shut the car door.

So there I was, wondering if something was wrong with the little guy's stereo. Or maybe guys this rich hired people to change records for them: "James, if you don't mind, old boy, Bach's Cantata in D minor." Maybe I'd get a uniform too. My mom always wanted to see me in a uniform—that is, when she didn't see me making millions of dollars as a personal injury attorney. One disappointed little woman, my mother. Oh well —so where were we?

We were walking up the flagstone path to the portico, my escort flapping his lips like there was no tomorrow. The sun was setting through the trees and a pinky glow surrounded the horizon.

"Here's what happens: you start out being pretty fluid, pretty flexible about time. You start hanging out in the dreams for fun. You start hanging out with your envisioned dreams—infinite in detail and complex—just like here."

I kind of tripped up the steps at this point, but he didn't notice.

"The only drawback in this solipsistic paradise is you know everything that's going to happen. That loses its novelty after a while."

The door opened and without breaking step, we entered the chandeliered anteroom to a palatial receiving room that seemed larger than the front of the house allowed for. It was a big, awesome place with marble floors and Persian rugs, crystal chandeliers and rooms leading into rooms like two mirrors facing each other. A yummy-looking maid with discreet manners and indiscreet legs shut the door after us and followed us into a library with a large statue of a dancing Vishnu with six or seven arms attached to a big halo. The maid shut the door and left us alone. I'd tried to catch her eye, but she wasn't looking. She was one luscious maid. The privileges of wealth.

My eccentric host sat behind a black granite desk and motioned for me to sit in an oblong contraption that passed for a chair. I noticed some music was filtering in from invisible speakers—it just seemed to be in the air. "Genius of Love" by the Tom Tom Club. "And the old coot's hip, to boot," I thought. Things just could not get any weirder.

"I'm not sure exactly when or how—" I was real glad to hear that, I mean at least the guy didn't know everything—"but at some point you start interacting your ideas with another fellow's ideas and you play around. Different fellows have different concepts of what's fun or what's admirable. Things don't necessarily go your way."

He kept talking, but he pulled a drawer open and pulled some sheets of paper out. He set them in front of him on the desk—white paper on black desk.

"Eventually you get in the habit of collecting up dreams you liked and dreams that opposed those dreams. These can continue to get activated every once in a while. If they get activated continuously, it's a continuous playing reality. If you're not conscious of it, it'll just keep on playing."

He picked up one of the pieces of paper and set it in front of me, another white rectangle on black desk, with three identical circles evenly spaced in black ink. I figured, great, maybe he is offering me a job and this is a sort of IQ test for record playback engineers. I hoped the maid fooled around.

"Which one is different?" he asked.

I looked them over. They were all the same.

"They're all the same."

He smiled. "Look again."

"But they're all the same," I objected.

He didn't seem to mind. "Just look them over and see if one feels different."

I looked, but the damn circles were absolutely identical. I figured my chances were one out of three, so I might as well make a stab at winning the prize. Besides, one of them did seem to have a bit of bluer black than the others.

I pointed to the second one. "This one."

The little man clapped his hands and cried, "Excellent!"

His records are probably color-coded, so he doesn't want any colorblind DJ's messing with his collection, I thought. I didn't believe that, I was just cracking wise to myself. What the hell would you do in the same circumstance? What would you do?

He got up and walked to the door. It opened before he got to it and the maid was there, but she'd changed into an indiscreetly low-cut, black, shimmering evening dress. A large diamond pendant sparkling just above the shadow of her cleavage. I liked that.

The little man waited for me in the hall. I got up and smiled at the maid. She smiled back. Now I'm getting someplace, I thought. She wandered off to a group of black tuxedos and evening dresses. There were people in them of course, smoking cigarettes and whispering, but I felt a little out of place in my Hawaiian shirt, blue jeans and tennis shoes, so that was all I saw.

We walked through a series of rooms until we arrived at a back porch the size of a ballroom floor. It was dark out; around the edges of the porch, clusters of elegantly dressed guests were flying kites. I thought it had been an oppressively windless day so I was wondering how they got the kites up in the air. Maybe the guy had a big set of fans tucked away someplace, like the hurricane fans they use in the movies.

My host walked up to one of these groups and took the kite string into his hands. A butler knelt beside him and held a stick with a large ball of string wound around it. I could not see the kite. It was up in the clouds someplace and it was dark. The little guy jerked the string a couple of times, like he was fishing, and a tongue of crackling scarlet flames shot up the string and into the clouds, then disappeared. The group of guests nodded appreciatively and my host handed the kite stick back to them.

That was six months ago. I got the job. They're all color-coded and I wear a black tuxedo. He's got a pretty good stereo system and a collection of records you would not believe. The three circles, you see, were absolutely identical. He just willed some blue into the one I picked.

Oh—I almost forgot. What about the nuclear holocaust? You're probably wondering what the hell does all this have to do with multi-warhead ICBM's.

Well, you see, it's like this:

The little man took me back inside. The maid led us back to the library again. I sat down on the oblong chair and he explained my duties as his record playback engineer. He walked over to the statue of Vishnu. I figured he was going to tell me he was Krishna or something, but he didn't.

"This reality," he said instead, "the set of individuals intermeshing to create this place, are involved with a particularly exciting and also dangerous set of dreams. There's an inevitable nuclear holocaust in the scheme of things if the activated dreams continue in the pattern they're in now. There's several million Indians, Chinese, Australian aborigines, and Appalachian people that haven't the slightest idea what a nuclear war is. They're all that stand between us and the holocaust. You see, enough intermeshing nightmares become reality, too—Hitler, Stalin, etc. So do a good job here and you may learn how to permute out of this place."

With that kind of incentive, and a couple of other conspicuous collateral benefits, I've given it my best shot. Karen, the maid, has been apprenticing me. I'm getting pretty good at it.

A nuclear holocaust is not the end of everything. Me, I may

hang around and watch the colors and all, then move onto another permutation. Karen tells me there's an Arthurian permutation not too hard to get to, Grail quests and all. So we're probably going to go there. But everyone who's fixated on this reality and can't permute, they'll have the unpleasant task of evolving up from chaos again. That's a damned unpleasant experience for individuals accustomed to something different. I mean spending a few hundred million years putting together a self-perpetuating organic molecule isn't exactly my idea of fun. They'll probably go absolutely unconscious from the boredom.

At any rate, things don't have to go that way, there's a lot of people trying to stop it and if I were you I'd at least participate in the "ban the bomb" groups. You may as well do something, for Christ's sake. There's a lot of different permutation stations around. Who knows, maybe it'll get postponed long enough. Stranger things have happened. That's all. Bye!

Saturday Afternoon at the Church of the Blessed Sacrament

ELAINE had passed the church innumerable times on the way home from work and had paid as little attention to it then as she had to the commercial buildings, billboards and deserted parking lots surrounding it. It was just another building mushed into the haze of objects pasted to her mind's eye at the end of a day. One time when she was caught in rush hour traffic, the church stood out in relief for a few minutes. She was in a hurry to get home and was extremely irritated that she was trapped in the middle of a block that had no smaller streets coming off it so she could get around the endless stretch of bumper-to-bumper cars. Her frustrated eyes wandered over the church's façade. There were what seemed like countless gray steps leading up to its towering colonnade. She decided to pass the time by counting them.

As she finished counting, she noticed that two of the front doors were wide open and she could see directly into the sanctuary. Looking through the doors gave her the illusion that the space within was larger than the building itself could possibly contain. It reminded her of a cartoon where Popeye walked into a sheik's tiny tent whose interior was an immense, luxurious palace. Cynically, she began wondering if the architects had consciously planned this sort of magical effect to dupe potential parishioners, but the traffic started moving again and she promptly forgot about architects, doors and churches.

It was nearly a year before she thought about the church again. It was a pleasant enough Saturday afternoon, but somehow she could not sit back and enjoy it. She had decided to stay home and relax for a change, but everywhere she went, there was some neglected responsibility bearing down on her. The kitchen sink was loaded with dishes, the living room was haunted by the project she had brought home from work, the sprawling mass of dirty clothes prevented her from taking a long, hot bath. And then there was the pile of unpaid bills stacked up on top of the TV. No matter where she went, there was something gnawing at her, and her apartment simply was not large enough to escape. Then she abruptly remembered the church doors and the illusion of spaciousness, and on an impulse she decided to drive down and take a closer look at them.

She parked on the street about a block away from the church. She was not really sure if it would even be open. She had read an article several years earlier about churches having to start locking their doors at night because their gold-laminated chalices and jewel-studded crosses had started disappearing. One church finally drew the line when someone had stolen the linen right off the altar. The inviolate sanctity of the Church had eroded bit by bit to the point that it was no longer immune to the pilferage to which its neighbors were subject. She climbed the steps preparing herself not to be disappointed if the doors were locked—nothing to take personally.

A smile edged across her face when she saw they were, in fact, open. She walked directly through the doors as if she were walking into a clothing store or a 7-Eleven. No furtive glances to see if anyone was watching her go in, no misgivings or trepidations about entering a church, a religious sanctuary. She did, however, pause at a counter laden with pamphlets, accompanied by a coin box for their purchase. She smirked again, not so much at the pamphlets' quaint titles (which did strike her as amusing), but at the double layer of price stickers on their upper right corners. *Nobody, not even the Church, escapes inflation*, she thought.

From there she wandered over to the doors leading to the central aisle of the church and was at once struck by the silence: no din of accelerating bus engines, no random horns blaring, no thump-thump of helicopters circling fugitives penetrated the thick layers of pious silence. She stood at the doorway, rather sentimentally touched by the aura of ancient holiness that permeated the entire interior of the place. The air even felt older. She shrugged it off after a few seconds and wondered if the building filtered out the city's smog as well as its distracting noises.

She did not care for churches because she generally did not care for sanctimonious religion which she found stuffy and confusing. She had not been in a church since she was thirteen or fourteen, not even for weddings. Any of her friends who had gotten married had done so outdoors or in hotel conference rooms. She entered the sanctuary noticing that much of the interior was just like the ones she remembered. There were the same sort of hand-carved wooden pews, the same sort of stained glass windows and arched ceiling, the same prayer books resting neatly in racks attached to the backs of the pews, rows of maroon velvet cushions to kneel on—all these things unchanged when so much had changed in and about her life. She felt a sense of stability and permanence as though she were in some sort of time warp that was immune to the progress of time. A sense of peace and awe passed over her which she suppressed as soon as she noticed it.

She sat down in one of the rear pews and looked about, observing the church with a sort of clinical, architectural interest. She glanced up at the ceiling and remembered it was supposed to look like the bottom of a boat. And it did. A great big Noah's Ark upside down. She wondered what part of the ship she was in, the fore or the aft or the prow. *Probably the poop deck*, she concluded sarcastically.

There were several chapels, almost as big as small churches, attached to either side of the nave. She supposed each one had a specific purpose: Monday masses, Chapel 1; Tuesday masses, Chapel 2; funerals for people with not very many friends, Chapel 3; christenings for small families, Chapel 4; and so on. There was one particularly pretty alcove with a life-size statue of Mary in it and a table with tiers of votive candles in front of her. The candles flickered inside their crimson, violet, yellow and cobalt stained glass containers, creating a rainbow-like milieu within an almost tangible goldness.

Elaine's chest released a long sigh. Here was a place so alien, so peacefully different from her life, from her style of existence, that she could relax and even close her eyes without fear of interruption. No phone could ring, no door could be knocked, no neighbor's stereo could sift through to annoy her. In the heart of the city she had found a sanctuary where she could do absolutely nothing.

A pair of plump elderly Mexican women wearing black dresses and scarves shuffled out of one of the nearby chapels. Elaine closed her eyes and hoped they would not say anything to her. She did not want to be sociable, to enter some category of social identity, to be obligated to smile, or to expect smiles. She wanted to be ignored. She listened to the click-clack of their shoes fading behind her and, again, she felt safe, but it was a safety amidst the emerging awareness that something in her life was amiss, something she could never have admitted to anyone, even herself, in other places, in other times.

It was not anything in particular that made her feel this way; it was just a general malaise, a psychic congestion. Her mind was inundated with billboard signs, dirty sidewalks, telephone wires, unkempt apartments and nuclear holocausts—the news and rock 'n' roll, unsatisfying linear relationships with men, the petrochemical poisoning of the aquifer, and Lord knew what else. It was all there waiting to assault her.

She sat motionless, with her eyes closed, flipping through thoughts and images. She did not have to flip through them, really. They were like a wound-up nickelodeon that only required her to let go of the spring-driven handle to break loose into fluid motion. Except they were from different movies so it was all disjointed. She thought if she sat there doing nothing long enough, they would eventually drop away. And bit by bit they did. Eventually there were spaces between pictures, not just a constant whirl. Then there was more space than images. The layers of suppressed emotions and avoided ideas—the billboards, smog and rot, the boyfriends and holocausts—just gently slipped away. She felt serene and uncongested. *I could stay like this a long time*, she thought.

At one point she recalled her confirmation. The swirl of incomprehension and embarrassment at being the focus of attention of hundreds of people, not being able to breathe, the figures of the priests and acolytes in their layers of cassocks and surplices. How awesome the bishop was as he turned around in his splendid, purple robe. A thick cloud of incense had swelled around her as the boat boy swung the censer at her again, and she felt like fainting. Then an immense hand emerged from beneath the purple sleeve, and the holy ring loomed in front of her. She'd kissed the ring and noticed its perfumed cleanliness through the fog of incense. She understood nothing of what had occurred, but when she recalled the hand coming at her face and the ring on her lips, a chill swept up and down her spine and she suddenly felt lighter.

She opened her eyes and the church seemed brighter. The light filtering through the stained glass windows was more colorful and intense. She felt a personal spaciousness not unlike the spaciousness of the church itself. She noticed again the resonant timelessness, the sense of something old and unadulterated despite hundreds of years of adulteration.

She closed her eyes again and felt as if she were in a clearing in a dense, towering forest. There were no altars or temples or statues. Just a shaft of light in the meadow-like clearing where she and several other people were basking in the sunlight, in some way conscious of an intuitive rapport, as if they were touching souls. It was this feeling that the church had reminded her of, that had drawn her there, that the church was a touchstone for. It did not matter what kind of church it was. It was just that it was quiet and spacious and timeless. That was enough.

Wrapped in this sensation, she rose slowly and glanced around, observing the chapels, stained glass windows and altar, the pews and confessional, absorbing their ambiance, feeling as if she were radiating out of her body and touching each thing she gazed upon. She smiled at the multi-colored votive candles flickering at Mary's feet and admired their gold glow. Then she turned and walked up the aisle and through the foyer.

Outside, the air was hot and thick with exhaust fumes from cars stuck in mid-day traffic. A dusty gray film layered the buildings and cars. A helicopter's blades thumped noisily overhead. A driver began sounding his horn. The billboards, sidewalk trash and telephone wires were still there. She knew her laundry, dishes and bills were still cluttering her apartment. As she started her car and began heading back home, none of it seemed as harsh or suffocating. Instead, she felt as if she were permeating into everything around her, like sunlight emanating through a layer of clouds.